The Spinster's Christmas

Lady Wynwood's Spies series
Prequel

Camille Elliot

Cover design by Dineen Miller/Designer Girl Graphics

Camy Tang
P.O. Box 23143
San Jose, CA 95153-3143
www.camilleelliot.com

Photo eBook: ISBN-13: 978-1-942225-02-7
Photo Print Book: ISBN-13: 978-1-942225-03-4
Illustrated eBook: ISBN-13: 978-1-942225-10-2
Illustrated Print Book: ISBN-13: 978-1-942225-09-6

To my readers:

My prayer for you is that you will know that God sees you and that you fully understand how much He loves you.

Lady Wynwood's Spies series

Recommended reading order

The Spinster's Christmas (prequel)

The Gentleman Thief (prequel novella)

Lady Wynwood's Spies, Volume 1: Archer

Lady Wynwood's Spies, Volume 2: Berserker

Lady Wynwood's Spies, Volume 3: Aggressor

Lady Wynwood's Spies, Volume 4: Betrayer

Lady Wynwood's Spies, Volume 5: Prisoner

Lady Wynwood's Spies, Volume 6: Martyr

Lady Wynwood's Spies, Volume 7: Spinster (coming soon)

Standalone novels

Prelude for a Lord

The Gentleman's Quest

Devotional

Who I Want to Be

And she called the name of the Lord that spake unto her, Thou God seest me: for she said, Have I also here looked after him that seeth me?

Genesis 16:13 (KJV)

And the peace of God, which passeth all understanding, shall keep your hearts and minds through Christ Jesus.

Philippians 4:7 (KJV)

Prologue

Dorsetshire, England, December 23rd, 1810

"I am heartily sick of your complaining and moaning, you old woman," Lady Wynwood told her companion, who was lounging on the seat across from her in her traveling coach.

The "old woman" was in actuality a fit man in his fourth decade, with a rugged face and an easy smile hovering on the edges of his mouth. His jaw might not be as firm as it had been twenty years ago, but he was still the handsome buck Laura had first met during her debut in London, and he knew it, too.

"Reduced to name-calling, Laura?" Solomon Drydale drawled.

"Would you rather I simply opened this coach door and booted you out of it?"

He grinned impudently at her in reply.

"You made the decision to ride inside the coach rather than alongside it on your horse," she continued. "Therefore, I do not wish to hear another groan about the springs of my axles or whatever it is that you call them. It is *my* coach, not yours."

Sol held up his hands in surrender. "You are quite right. Forgive me." He gave her that charming half-smile that never failed to soften the ire of the most peevish of dowagers.

Laura rolled her eyes.

The coach jolted again on the badly potted road. Laura set her teeth.

Sol groaned at the jolt. "How much farther to Wintrell Hall?" In response to her black look, he quickly added, "I am not complaining. It is a sincere question."

"You have been to Wintrell Hall before."

"It has been a year or two since I accompanied you to Sir Cecil's home for Christmastide," Sol said. "I am hardly required to remember the length of each stage of the journey."

"We are nearly on Cecil's lands," Laura said.

"Good." Sol settled deeper into the plush velvet seat. "Sir Cecil Belmoore may be an insufferable prig, but at least he is responsible enough to see to the upkeep of his roads."

"Solomon Drydale," Laura said in shocked accents. "Remember you are speaking of my cousin's son."

"Oh, for goodness' sake, you like the man as little as I do."

She gave a disgusted sound. "You are incorrigible."

"Since when have you been too reticent to speak your mind with me?" he demanded. "It is only the two of us in this rattling—er, splendidly sprung coach."

"I knew you were not overly fond of Sir Cecil, but I had no idea you disliked him so much. If such is the case, you could have chosen to spend the season with your own family," she said pointedly.

Sol didn't answer, but his face took on a grim cast.

Laura eyed him. "What unpleasantness are you avoiding in so cowardly a fashion?"

Her goad hit its mark. "It is hardly cowardly to wish to avoid the machinations of a desperate woman."

She raised her eyebrows at him.

Sol sighed. "You are not the only one to have relations who wish to marry you off to their person of choice. In my case, my sister-in-law has hopes for her niece or cousin or some sort."

Laura's laugh hopefully hid the pang that squeezed her heart at his words. She oughtn't to be surprised. Solomon Drydale was an eligible widower with a vast estate, and great-grandson to a viscount. "I would think you would be up to the tricks of a young girl."

"She's not young, she's nearly thirty."

"A veritable babe," Laura said with narrowed eyes. She herself was now on the disagreeable side of forty.

Sol simply smiled at her. "Have no fear. You, my dear, are still as youthful as the day I met you in Green Park."

He delivered his compliments with that quirk to his lips that made the dimple peek out from his left cheek. But she refused to count herself among the scores of other widows in London who were half in love with him. "Are you now a merchant trading in Spanish coin? You are not usually so flattering to me, Sol."

"Not flattering, merely answering your question. Avoiding Miss Whatever-her-name is the reason I chose to spend Christmastide with you and your Belmoore relations. Our reasons are not so dissimilar."

He was right. On Laura's father's side of the family,

her cousin's wife, Matilda, had a profligate brother with a penchant for gambling. Matilda had already attempted some rather devious plots to bring Laura into company with him, perhaps even to orchestrate a scandalous situation that would force Laura to marry the gambler. So Laura was avoiding her father's relations this year in favor of the Belmoores, her mother's side of the family.

"I do hope there are no Matildas among the family party," Sol said. "Your late cousin was not clever enough to be so devious, so I am assuming his son, Sir Cecil, is the same."

"Sol, you imp," Laura admonished him. "You are trying to make me confess my family members' faults, but the truth is that I like them a great deal."

"I seem to recall your complaining to me about some rather priggish letters Sir Cecil sent to you regarding how you administered your fortune," Sol said.

In other words, Sir Cecil had disliked the fact that Laura had control of her own money. Laura had ignored the letters. Sol had laughed at them, but he had no great regard for Sir Cecil, the present head of the Belmoore family.

"You like my cousin Edward," she reminded him. "And I assure you that his sisters have much more countenance now than when you met them during their come-outs." They now had children and even grandchildren. The thought of their families made her smile. She adored all the children who gathered for Christmas at Wintrell Hall and looked forward to the games and charades.

"Now what has brought that brightness to your lovely face?" Sol asked.

She hesitated because she knew her answer would pain him. "I was thinking about the Christmas games. With the children."

He smiled in response, although it did not reach his eyes. "That is because you are so competitive."

"Now I know you are back to your normal self, because you are dishing up rude remarks once more," she said.

"I must take heed of my tongue, lest I offend some matron and turn Christmastide into a theatrical tragedy."

"I am not concerned about your tongue."

"Are you not? And they being your family?"

"However much you play the churl with me, you would never forget yourself in company."

"Now who's dealing in Spanish coin?"

"However, you will be looking for any opportunity to goad *me* into saying something offensive," Laura continued.

Sol grinned. "Because it is so much fun when you do."

Laura glared. It had only been the once when she'd been indiscreet enough to say out loud that she thought Lady Adderly's hat looked like a molting chicken. She said in a firm tone, "I wish for a happy, uneventful Christmastide this year." Unspoken was her admonition, *Behave, Sol.*

"Yes, yes." Sol grinned at her. "Completely uneventful, I assure you."

Chapter One

December 23rd

Captain Gerard Foremont, lately of His Majesty's Royal Navy, wasn't certain what caused him to notice the woman walking on the road toward Wintrell Hall. When he spotted the slim figure in a dark green wool cloak, something about the tilt of her head, the cadence of her measured stride, triggered a memory.

He had been fourteen years old, about to leave home as a midshipman on his uncle's frigate and spending a last Christmas with the Belmoores, old family friends, here at Wintrell Hall. They'd been hauling mistletoe and greenery when twelve-year-old Miranda had come up to him, raising her head. As always, he was momentarily startled by her crystal-green eyes framed by dark lashes. He rarely saw her eyes because she usually kept her head lowered.

"Will you miss us, when you are at sea?" she asked.

"Of course I will," he said as they walked toward the house.

"Christmas won't be the same without you. You make

us all laugh. Even Cecil."

Gerard laughed at that. "Then you must learn what will make our stodgy Cecil laugh more. Come, Miranda. I want some hot punch, don't you?"

The memory faded as his family's coach came up on the woman in the green cloak. She raised her head to look at him, and he caught the flash of crystal green.

"Stop the coach!" he ordered. The coachman heard him and began reining in the horses.

"Whatever for?" his mother asked.

"It's Miranda. We should offer her a lift to the house."

Gerard's mother and father exchanged a strange look. Then his mother said, "Have we room for her?" She didn't quite gesture toward the stout cane propped between the seats and leaning against the corner of the coach.

Gerard's forehead tightened, not solely from the reminder of the cane, but also in shock at his mother's want of hospitality. "What?"

His father said to his mother, "Dear, the coach has already stopped. It would appear odd if we did not offer her a ride."

"Oh. Yes, of course," his mother said.

Gerard automatically reached for the door handle ... then remembered in time that he'd have too much difficulty climbing out.

His father pretended he hadn't seen the gesture, and said heartily, "I'll go out and fetch the girl, shall I?" He tossed aside the blankets warming his legs, opened the door and stepped outside, raising his hand to hail her. "Miranda! My dear, walking in this weather? Come inside the coach with us."

"Thank you, Mr. Foremont," said a low voice. However, it did not sound like the Miranda he knew. He'd only seen her a few times in the sixteen years since he'd gone to sea, and the last time had been almost three years ago, before her parents had died and she'd gone to live with her cousin, Sir Cecil Belmoore. Miranda had always been quiet, but this voice sounded ... defeated.

Her figure appeared in the doorway, but he couldn't see her face, obscured by her bonnet. His father handed her into the coach, and she looked up at Gerard.

Crystal green pierced him, and elation rushed through him, pulsing with his heartbeat. He couldn't breathe. He wanted to reach out to touch her, to have some point of connection, and so he did, taking her hand. He squeezed her fingers. He didn't want to release her.

She dropped into the seat across from him, her eyes lowered once again. He was forced to relinquish her hand.

He tried to speak, but found he had to clear his throat twice before he could say, "It's good to see you again, Miranda."

"You look well, Gerard," she said.

"Not quite at death's door," he said in a light tone.

"I do wish you would stop exaggerating your injury, Gerard," his mother said tartly.

Miranda sent her a surprised look, but Gerard had become used to his mother's frayed temper in the past few months. She was not gifted in the sickroom, and being forced to care for her son had become wearisome for her. She loved him, he knew that, but she loved him more when he was whole and not in need of constant care.

"Miranda, my dear, why were you out today?" Gerard's father asked. "It's quite cold to be walking."

"I had an errand to run for Felicity in the village," Miranda said.

"That was kind of you," Gerard said. However, the words she used made it sound as though the errand had been expected of her rather than as a favor to her cousin's wife.

Sitting next to Gerard, his mother cleared her throat. His father said to Miranda, "Are you warm enough? Here, take this brick for your feet. It is still warm."

"No, I am perfectly well." Miranda's voice had that same serenity that he remembered, which soothed over awkward moments and calmed crying children.

His father insisted, moving his warmed brick from beneath his feet to Miranda's. It was then that Gerard noticed her clothes. He was not one to notice women's clothing very often, but because of his mother's fastidious taste, he understood the standards of dress worn by the women of his class.

However, the leather of Miranda's half-boots was old and cracked, in worse shape than the boots in which he used to walk the fields with his father. He then noticed the frayed edge of her gown and the faded blue of the thin wool fabric. Her cloak, too, was worn at the bottom edge and where it fastened at her throat. And compared to his mother's bonnet, crisp straw lined with velvet, Miranda's bonnet was limp and crushed, with her dark hair escaping in smooth strands. The ribbons tied under her chin were wrinkled and old, more suited for summer than winter.

Miranda looked like ...

"Ellie will be happy to see you, ma'am," Miranda said to his mother. "She was asking after you all this week, wondering when you would arrive."

The mention of the six-year-old made his mother smile. "We so enjoyed her visit in the summer. It quite lifted my spirits."

Her joyful tone contrasted with her peevishness with her own son, and Gerard looked away. But he could not fault her. An orphaned grand-niece was surely better company than an invalid sailor.

This past summer, Ellie had been sent to visit her mother's relations at Foremont Court. Because Gerard's mother loved children, she'd begged Ellie's grandfather to extend the visit to a full eight weeks. At the time, Gerard had still been in the hospital in London, recovering from the cannonball that had exploded the deck beneath his feet, driving splintered wood into his knee.

Only when Gerard had been about to return home was his mother forced to give up Ellie and let her go back to the household of Sir Cecil, her father's cousin. Ellie's paternal grandfather had not felt adequate to raise a young girl after her father had been killed on the Peninsula and her mother had died in childbirth only a few months later, so Ellie had been living with Cecil's family above eight months now.

"How is Ellie?" Gerard's mother asked Miranda.

Miranda hesitated before answering. "She was in high spirits in the weeks after she returned from your home, but since then, she has become quieter. It is difficult for her since Cecil's two younger boys are away at school most of the year, and only his two older daughters are at home. They are more likely to want to talk about gowns and fripperies than romp about with Ellie."

"She has no playmates in the neighborhood?" Gerard asked.

Miranda said carefully, "Cecil is fastidious about the company his family keeps."

Gerard frowned. Cecil apparently hadn't changed in the years since they'd all played together. He was likely too proud to want to associate with any families of insufficiently high birth.

"Ellie enjoyed playing with our neighbors' children. There was a veritable herd of children that galloped into our drawing room for tea and biscuits every morning," his mother said with a laugh.

Because unlike Cecil, Gerard's family had good relationships with all their neighbors, who had many young children below the age of ten.

"I worry that she is lonely," Miranda said.

"You mustn't worry," Gerard said. "After Twelfth Night, we plan to take Ellie home with us to stay."

He caught a flash of green as she raised her head, and her mouth fell open. "You do?"

"We should enjoy having Ellie with us ever so much," his mother said. "The idea would never have come into our heads if we had not met Lady Wynwood in London a month ago. It was she who suggested it. She had recently spoken to her cousin Edward—Ellie's grandfather—and he had mentioned that Ellie was feeling low."

"Laura thought Ellie would enjoy a change of scenery," his father said, "with the added benefit of having a girl around the house to cheer Mary up." He patted his wife's hand.

"It will not occupy too much of your time with Gerard to have Ellie at your home?" Miranda had always been rather blunt, but the artless way she said it made it obvious that she was concerned about him.

Gerard had had enough of pity from his family and neighbors in the past few months, but somehow Miranda's concern did not upset him. "I am well on the mend. In fact, I insisted we convince Uncle Edward to allow us to take Ellie."

"Uncle Edward agreed to it?" Miranda asked. "Cecil's house is but ten miles from his own."

"And Foremont Court is merely twelve in the other direction," his father said. "Ellie will be able to see her grandfather as often as she wishes."

"Does Cecil know of this plan?" Miranda asked. Gerard wondered if anyone besides himself could hear the wary edge to her voice.

"Not yet," his father said.

"I can't imagine why he should make a fuss at having a dependent taken off his hands," his mother said. "Cecil may be the tenth Baronet Belmoore, but Edward is Cecil's uncle and Ellie's grandfather, and her legal guardian."

"And both of Ellie's grandfathers agree to the plan," Gerard's father said, "for not only Edward, but also my brother have written their consent."

"It would be better by far for Ellie to remove to your home," Miranda agreed.

At this point, the coach turned onto the stretch of drive that led up to the front of Wintrell Hall. The trees lining the drive were bare, but snow had not yet fallen, and the lawn in front of the house was a pale ash-green color. In contrast, on the east side of the house, the bushes peeking over the top of the stone garden wall were a startling orange-brown, waving in the wind that swept down the valley and swirled around the house.

They weren't the first to arrive, for as they passed the red brick stables, a coachman was directing the grooms and stablehands in maneuvering a massive traveling coach inside the building.

They pulled up in front of the north entrance, and the butler and a footman promptly came out to meet them. In the winter sunlight, the red brick of the house was a warm russet color, which belied the blast of cold wind that rushed into the coach when the servant opened the door. "Welcome, Mr. and Mrs. Foremont, Captain Foremont," said the butler. His gray eyebrows rose slightly at the sight of Miranda in the coach, but that was the extent of how he showed his surprise.

"Thank you, Lewis," Mrs. Foremont said as the butler helped her alight. "Have Cecil's sisters arrived with their families?"

"Yes, ma'am. And their husbands' families, as well."

Gerard's mother gave a happy sigh. "The nursery must be full to bursting."

"And eagerly awaiting your arrival, if I may say so, ma'am," Lewis unbent enough to say.

Gerard gestured for Miranda to precede him out of the coach, but she shook her head violently.

"Miranda, what is going on?" he whispered to her.

Her only answer was to say in a neutral tone, "I shall pass you your cane, Captain Foremont."

Gerard gritted his teeth at the necessity of being assisted from the coach by his father and the footman. A year ago, he would have ...

Best not to think of it.

He had just taken his cane from Miranda when Felicity, Lady Belmoore, came out to greet them. "Mr. and Mrs. Foremont, you are come at last. And Gerard, you are looking well." Her smile froze before it reached her blue eyes. "How good of you to give Miranda a lift to the house, but quite unnecessary of you."

"Whyever not?" Gerard said with a touch of belligerence. "Miranda is hardly a scullery maid."

"It is my fault entirely," his father interjected. "Miranda demurred, but I insisted when I heard she was returning from an errand. We have brought her home sooner in case she should be needed."

"So kind of you," Felicity said. "Come inside, out of this wind. There's tea in the drawing room."

Miranda followed everyone into the house, but Gerard caught the disapproving look that Felicity shot toward her.

He was careful in climbing the stairs, his good leg beginning to shake with the strain from the two flights of the grand staircase. By the time he'd finally reached the drawing room with his parents and Felicity, Miranda had disappeared.

He lowered himself into a gold and white striped chair, but his leg gave out and he fell heavily into the seat, making it wobble on its delicately carved legs. He winced. *Yes, Gerard, the quickest way to cultivate Cecil's good graces is to break his furniture.*

Felicity's eyes widened slightly, but when the chair

held, she relaxed.

"Gerard, I would not have thought the stairs to be so cumbersome for you," his mother said critically.

He had been used to his commanders shouting in his face, but his mother's impatience with his slow rate of recovery had worn through his temper like a taut length of rope being slowly shredded by friction. He was tempted to reply with some caustic remark, but held his tongue in front of Felicity.

Ever the peacemaker, his father said, "I wonder, Felicity, if we could beg your indulgence. Perhaps it would be best to give Gerard a room on this floor?"

"Oh, it would be no trouble at all," she said.

Gerard pressed his lips together briefly before answering politely, "Thank you, I would be most appreciative."

"If you will excuse me a moment to speak to my servants." Felicity rose and left the drawing room.

Gerard took advantage of the moment of privacy to lean closer to his parents. "What is going on with respect to Miranda?" he demanded in a low voice.

His parents looked at each other, that uncanny way they could communicate without speaking.

"Would you rather discuss this with Felicity here?" Gerard asked.

His mother sighed. "So awkward."

"What is?"

"Miranda's position in this household," she said.

"I don't understand. She's Cecil's cousin."

"Her parents died in great debt," his father said. "Their tenant farms had been in decline for years and the house was mortgaged to the hilt. Cecil was forced to settle their obligations with the bank, and then to take Miranda into his household."

Gerard could imagine how Cecil had felt about that. He was scrupulous with his money, to the point that he was a bit of a nip-farthing even though his wealth was substantial. It would have been painful for him to part with so much of his blunt to pay his uncle's debts.

"Felicity was not best pleased," his mother said. "She and Miranda have never gotten along."

"But I don't understand why—"

"I apologize," Felicity said as she sailed back into the room. "It is so difficult to find good servants these days. They never seem to understand what you wish them to do. Could I pour you more tea, Mrs. Foremont?"

At that moment, the door opened again and Cecil's aunt, Mrs. Augusta Hathaway, burst into the room. "John and Mary, I have only just heard you were arrived. How lovely to see you. And little Gerard!" She did not wait for him to struggle to his feet, but bent to kiss his cheek, enveloping him in her expensive French perfume. "You are looking so well."

"Hardly little any longer, Mrs. Hathaway," Gerard said.

"You will always be little to me, no matter how you grow." Mrs. Hathaway plopped herself down upon the sofa. "You must tell me how you all have been doing. Felicity, be a dear and pour me a cup of tea. I am parched after settling the children in the nursery."

"Oh, you must tell me how your granddaughters are," his mother said. "I have not seen them since last Christmas."

Gerard said little as the others talked. He was not

skilled at waiting, but it seemed he must wait for an explanation of what had happened to Miranda for her to be treated so differently by her own family. It upset him. His own extended Foremont relations would not have treated a poor relation so shabbily.

His father had been good friends with Edward Belmoore, Sir Cecil's uncle and Ellie's grandfather, since they were schoolboys together, which was why the Foremonts were always invited to Wintrell Hall for the elaborate Christmas celebrations. He was friendly with the Belmoores, but he had sometimes disagreed with the way the family conducted themselves in their relationships with others.

He disliked the little that he understood about the goings-on here. He thought of the men who had died under his command, and the injuries he had suffered. What had they all fought for when there was still such injustice at home?

Chapter Two

"Miranda." Felicity's sharp, displeased voice echoed harshly from the wainscoting along the walls of the nursery wing's corridor.

Miranda stopped on her way to her room and turned. Felicity stood at the head of the stairs. Waiting for her to come to her.

She headed back down the hallway. "What is it, Felicity?"

Felicity gave an impatient huff and strode to meet Miranda halfway. "For goodness' sake, you walk as slowly as a slug."

Miranda's mother had complained of that, as well, but she and others among the Belmoores had equated Miranda's slowness of foot with slowness of mind, also. Probably because in moments like these, Miranda simply said nothing. It made others uncomfortable, which was why Miranda did it.

Felicity waited, and when the silence stretched on, she blinked several times before saying, "I only needed to tell you that we won't be needing your presence at dinner tonight. We are already even at table, because there are a few guests who will be arriving tomorrow."

Miranda kept her eyes lowered as her hands fisted in the fabric of her skirts. "Of course," she said evenly.

"But do come to me in the drawing room after dinner. I might need you. And what do you mean by accepting a ride in Mr. Foremont's carriage? I was ever so embarrassed that they'd seen you in that shabby gown."

"I had thought you would want the ribbons I fetched for you a half hour sooner."

Felicity's lips pursed. They barely cracked open as she said, "Very well. But do try to spare a thought for my feelings. The less you are noticed, the better."

Miranda felt as if she had been plunged into the lake. Her hands began to shake, making the fabric of her gown tremble.

"It will be better for all of us when you go to my cousin Polly's household after Twelfth Night," Felicity added.

"Felicity, I beg you to reconsider sending me," Miranda said. Her hands now trembled with a darker emotion than mortification. "One of the maids has told me that there are ... rumors about Mr. Beatty. The people who live near the Beattys spoke of maids who ran away from their posts."

"Polly has always had difficulty retaining her nursery servants," Felicity said impatiently. "It is the reason I am sending *you*."

"But the maid said there were some indelicate stories. Two of the maids were thought to be pregnant, and a third killed herself."

"Miranda!" Felicity's cheeks flamed with color. "Listening to spurious gossip—nay, repeating it!"

As an unmarried young woman, it was highly improper of Miranda to say these things, but she had to try to make Felicity see the truth and change her mind. "Villagers nearby will not allow their daughters to work at the Beatty home, no matter what the wages are. Felicity, do you not understand?"

"I understand that you are being disobliging," Felicity snapped. "After we have taken you into our home, for you to go and serve my cousin is the least you could do."

Miranda would be an unpaid servant in a household with a man rumored to have a penchant for forcing the maids. "Please, Felicity," she said.

"I will hear no more of such horrid lies about my cousin's husband," Felicity said. "Cecil would be shocked if I were to tell him what you have said to me, you ungrateful wretch of a girl." In an angry whirlwind of skirts, Felicity left Miranda standing alone in the nursery wing corridor.

Was she ungrateful? Were the rumors untrue? And yet her cousin's wife should be more concerned about the possible danger to her relation, even if she was not connected by blood.

Miranda squeezed her eyes shut, all her limbs fluttering like leaves in a stiff winter wind. Life here with Felicity was difficult, but she simply could not go to the Beattys. She must find a way to save herself.

She shivered violently. She had been in the stillroom, which was pleasantly warm from the heat of the kitchen next to it. However, this wing of the house had terrible drafts, and so she went to her room to collect a shawl. She exerted herself to calm her jumbled emotions.

As she exited the room, she nearly collided with a

large male figure. She had been too preoccupied even to hear his footsteps.

There was a clatter of wood upon the floor, and then warm hands clasped her shoulders. She caught a whiff of sea rushes and mint and knew without looking that it was Gerard. He had not touched her like this since they'd played together as children, and she remained perfectly still, not wanting him to release her.

"Miranda, what are you doing?" He peered at the governess's room behind her. "Why were you in there?"

"It is where I am sleeping for the holidays, since we are full to the rafters with guests."

"In the nursery maid's room?"

"No, I am sharing the governess's room. We have no nursery maid."

He frowned at her as his hands dropped from her shoulders. "Surely Cecil can afford one?"

"He has no need of one while I am here."

His face grew dark. "He ought not to treat you this way. You are his cousin."

"I am a poor relation now, Gerard. That is how poor relations are treated."

"Not all poor relations are treated this way."

"Did you expect an outpouring of love from Cecil or Felicity?"

His eyes, the color of cinnamon, narrowed as they surveyed her. "Who is in your bedroom, then?"

"The nursery maids that Aunt Augusta and Aunt Anne brought with them."

His brows furrowed. "*Maids?* In your bedroom?"

It took her a moment to understand his outrage, and she quickly said, "My bedroom is not in the family wing of the house. It is there." She pointed to the door opposite.

But it seemed to make him even more shocked and angered on her behalf. "Do you mean to say that you sleep in the nursery maid's room?"

"It's closer to Ellie's bedroom, and to the younger boys when they are home on holiday from school. I don't mind."

"Miranda ..."

"Ellie needs me sometimes in the middle of the night. She still misses her mama—it's been barely a year since Beth died. And I can give her the kind of attention that no stranger would give to her." She added, "I don't wish for you to become upset on my account."

To forestall his reply, she bent to pick up his cane. He'd dropped it when he'd grabbed her to prevent her from running into him. "Here you are. Soon you will no longer need it."

He held her gaze, and she couldn't look away. He was aware of her attempts to change the subject, but he acquiesced. "I suppose I should be grateful I can stand without aid now, but it is still frustrating to need this." He set the foot of the cane on the wooden floor with a sharp snap.

He would never know the agonies she had suffered, praying fervently for him each night when she had first heard about the severity of his injuries from a letter his father had sent to her uncle Edward.

"Are you here to see Ellie?" she asked.

"Yes. I can hear the noise from the nursery all the way down the staircase."

"All the children are excited to be with their cousins

again."

"I recall we were that way, at their age."

She had lived for the times when he had joined their large family gatherings. His father's close friendship with her uncle Edward had enabled him nearly to grow up with her and her cousins, at least until he went to sea. He had never known how much she cared for him, how she had pined for him with girlish tears. She was a girl no longer, but she still felt remnants of that wistful longing for him, that little gasp of excitement in her chest when he looked at her.

Gerard would never know. He must never know.

"The children are eating dinner at the moment," she said. "Perhaps if you visited them later tonight?"

"When have I ever stood on ceremony with the brats? I'll pop in to say hello, wrestle a few of them to the ground, and make them cast up their accounts." He grinned. "I shall see you at dinner, then."

She considered giving a noncommittal answer because she knew the unvarnished truth would upset him again, but he would know the truth eventually. "I will not be downstairs. I am having dinner in the nursery."

He had been about to head toward the nursery but he stopped. His cane halted in midair for a split second before it snapped down on the floor again. "Why would you do that?"

She bit her tongue so that she would not say the first thing that came to mind, namely, *Felicity is exercising her ability to count heads at table.*

However, the expression on her face must have given her away, because he said incredulously, "Felicity has barred you from the dining room?"

"Nothing quite so barbaric. You know how fanatically she values order and appearances. She does not wish an odd number of guests at table tonight."

Gerard's face grew thunderous. "That is outside of enough."

"Gerard, I shall not be missed in the least." While she knew it was true, saying it out loud seemed to hammer it into her chest with a hollow blow. No one would notice her absence, and indeed, some members of the party would even welcome it.

Her words seemed to have shocked him. Finally he sputtered, "Of course you will be missed. We all grew up together. It would not be the same without you there." He checked himself, then added, "You and everyone else, of course."

The spark of warmth that had involuntarily risen at his words was doused by the splash of reality. Gerard had never looked at her as other than a friend, and surely by now, after years apart, she had outgrown her childish infatuation with him. She gave him a rueful smile to hide her feelings. "Gerard, when have you known me to speak more than a dozen words at table? No one will pine for my brilliant conversational *bon mots*."

A flicker of a smile on his face. "I want it all to be as it was the year before I went to sea. I have looked forward to Christmas in England these many years past."

There was an echo of longing in his voice, and she could imagine what his Christmases had been like on his ship, far from home and family.

"I shall speak to Felicity," he said.

"Pray, do *not*," she said fervently.

"She is treating you like a servant."

"Because we have never gotten along and she is resentful that Cecil was forced to take me in. If you insist I sit at dinner, she will do something else."

"It is not right, Miranda."

"There is nothing you can ..." An idea suddenly formed in her mind, vague like the sun straining to shine through mist over the fields, but slowly gaining strength. And hope.

"Miranda?" he asked.

"Do you wish to help me?"

"Of course. Name it."

"Will you speak to your mother on my behalf? Will you ask if she will consent to allow me to travel to Foremont Court with Ellie after Twelfth Night?"

He sighed. "You saw my mother's temper in the carriage," he said in a low voice. "She is not best pleased with me. I fear I could not sway her."

"Please, would you try? Ellie is very attached to me. You would have no need to hire a nursery maid."

His dark brows drew low over his eyes. "Miranda, I will not have you treated like a poor relation at our home, as well."

"Gerard, my situation is intolerable." She could not bring herself to speak such disgraceful gossip about Mr. Beatty to a young man—and certainly not Gerard—but she was desperate. Even admitting her desperation to him was difficult for her, who had always had to take care of herself.

A step on the stair made them both turn to see one of the under-maids, Jean, appear at the top of the stairs.

She gave Miranda and Gerard a saucy, appraising look. Jean always seemed reluctant to serve Miranda or Miss Teel, the governess, and Miranda had the impression that Jean resented their place in the household, neither fish nor fowl, as it were—neither genteel nor of the servant class.

"What is it?" Miranda said, a bit shortly.

"Lady Belmoore requires you to fetch her rose-embroidered petticoat from her room and repair it before tomorrow."

That was a task for Felicity's abigail. "What about Hobson?" Miranda asked.

"She has to alter some fancy gown for milady at the last minute and is too busy."

"Very well." Miranda nodded to Jean, but the girl lingered at the top of the stairs, regarding Gerard with obvious interest.

He cleared his throat. "Thank you, that will be all."

Jean's mouth pinched, but she turned to walk back down the stairs.

"I am shocked at the forwardness of Felicity's servants," Gerard said.

"It is only Jean, I assure you. Felicity runs a *tight ship*."

He laughed. "Just so." He hesitated, then said, "I will speak to my mother, Miranda. But I do not wish to falsely raise your hopes."

She realized that in those short moments, she had begun to rely upon Gerard. No, that would never do. She had long ago learned that it was futile to rely on anyone else besides herself.

He suddenly reached out and grabbed her hand.

Neither of them wore gloves, and she felt the calluses of his fingers, the warmth of his palm. Somehow, his touch made her feel more substantial than she usually did in this household. He knew her, he saw her, where everyone else tried to forget her. She realized she had been growing accustomed to the feeling of having lost her identity.

"I meant what I said," Gerard said. "I am happy to see you. For me, you are part of the Christmas season."

She smiled and turned to go downstairs to Felicity's room while he continued toward the nursery. But his words had caused a twinge in her chest, like a harp string too harshly plucked.

His anger on her behalf had made her feel less alone, and his kindness was a balm to her spirit after two years under Felicity's thumb. But in truth, Gerard and his family would leave after Twelfth Night, and Miranda would be sent to Felicity's cousin's home.

She could only rely on herself to save herself.

Chapter Three

For the better part of the last ten minutes, Gerard had been staring up Cecil's hairy nostrils. It was most unpleasant, but Cecil had kept his nose upturned during their entire discussion here in the library, which had taken place directly after dinner. Gerard wondered that Cecil didn't get a crick in his neck from looking down at all the world. Or perhaps Cecil simply had extraordinarily large nostrils.

"I assure you it is no hardship for Eleanor to continue her stay here," Sir Cecil said, playing with a pretentiously large silver paperweight upon his desk. "She is firmly fixed in our home. Indeed, the entire neighborhood is aware of it and approves."

Ah, now Gerard understood. Cecil would never admit it, but he did not want it known that he had "cast out" a little girl dependent upon him, especially because he obviously had the means to continue to keep her. It might reflect poorly upon his reputation, which was not otherwise known for its generosity.

"Surely you would not object to such a small sacrifice on your part for my mother's health and happiness?"

Gerard asked.

Cecil blinked rapidly, unable to think of a suitable response.

Gerard's father turned to Mr. Belmoore, Ellie's grandfather, who sat in an overstuffed chair. "Mary has always loved children, and they love her. She has always wanted a girl."

"In addition to her most excellent son," Gerard added with a grin. Mr. Belmoore returned it, but Cecil sniffed.

"We have the added advantage of more children of Ellie's age in our neighborhood than there are around Wintrell Hall," Gerard's father said.

Seeing Cecil's brows draw low, Gerard added, "I assure you they are all of *good* family."

Cecil said nothing, obviously thinking better of calling the statement into question because it would be insulting to Gerard's father.

"Cecil, you recall I expressed some concern on that head a few months ago," Mr. Belmoore said to his nephew. "John is perfectly right. Ellie would have more playmates if she were to go with him. She has been lonely and of low spirits since her mother died." Mr. Belmoore reached over to clap Gerard on the shoulder. "My only real concern, dear boy, is your health."

"I'm strong as an ox. Don't let the cane fool you. Come, I'll wrestle you, and you'll see."

Mr. Belmoore laughed. "I don't doubt your enthusiasm, but I simply wish to be assured that you are recovered enough to have a lively young girl underfoot."

"I have improved considerably, or I would not have put forward this scheme."

"Are you ... completely recovered?" Mr. Belmoore

asked.

Gerard knew what he was asking. "The doctor tells me that I shall walk with this cane for many months yet, perhaps years. But a full recovery is entirely within my grasp."

"Years?" Cecil said. "And what manner of accidents may befall a child? That cane is downright dangerous."

"I hardly intend to bat at her like a cricket pitch," Gerard protested.

"No one is accusing you of anything of the sort," Mr. Belmoore said, "but Gerard, I speak from experience when I say that a young girl Ellie's age can be dangerously unpredictable, especially for a man with difficulties getting about." He took his walking stick from where it leaned against his chair and tapped his left foot. "My gout has its good and bad days, but after Edmund died in action and Beth and Ellie came to stay with me, I had any number of accidents. Ellie likes to run, and will often run into things like legs, even when she does not intend to do so."

Yes, Gerard had seen Ellie running about earlier this evening before their dinner in the nursery, darting here and there. She and the other children had not sat down to behave themselves until Miranda had arrived in the room half an hour later, restoring order.

But he disliked the caution in Mr. Belmoore's tone. Gerard was a sailor who had fought, and he'd had enough of being treated like a porcelain figurine or a gouty old man. "I assure you, sir, I will have no difficulties with Ellie. I quite look forward to playing with her." The memory of the nursery also reminded him of his promise to Miranda, and he turned to his father.

"Sir, I have not had opportunity to speak to you of this, but I thought we might take Miranda with us, if only for a few months, to assist Mother with Ellie."

His father looked thoughtful. "That may be a good plan, although you will need to persuade your mother. And obtain Cecil's permission, naturally." He inclined his head toward Cecil.

Cecil frowned. "It matters not to me what happens to *Miranda*."

His tone made Gerard's teeth grind together.

Cecil continued, "However, Felicity had hoped to send the girl to her cousin's home after Twelfth Night. They have lost yet another nursery maid."

Gerard had expected Cecil to object to losing his unpaid servant, but this unexpected need of his wife's close relation would perhaps take precedence over Gerard's family.

"Cecil, you must order your household as you think best," Mr. Belmoore said. "As for Ellie, I have decided she will go to the Foremonts at the end of the Christmas celebrations."

"Thank you, sir." As Gerard shook Mr. Belmoore's hand, he determined to spend every moment that he could playing with Ellie within sight of her grandfather, to show him that his injury was not affected in the slightest by having a child about. Regardless, he would need Ellie to become accustomed to him. She had been shy when he'd introduced himself in the nursery earlier.

He desperately hoped that having Ellie's company would improve his mother's temperament, which was wearing on both himself and his father. He had brought such difficulties to them because of his injury, and he only wanted to make his mother happy again.

They all returned to the drawing room. One of the cousins was pounding away at the pianoforte while some of the furniture at the far end of the room had been rearranged to clear space for a few couples to dance.

Gerard sank into a chair near his mother, while his father sat beside her on the sofa.

"All went as expected, my dear," his father said to her. "Ellie shall come home with us when we leave."

His mother gasped with delight and clasped her husband's hands in her own. "How wonderful it will be to have Ellie with us. The house has been so gloomy lately."

Gerard looked away, but found he was staring down at his injured leg. At the very least, Ellie would distract his mother from the task of nursing him, which she had come to resent more in the past few weeks.

"The village seamstress is not as skilled as Madame Fanchon in London, but Ellie must have a new wardrobe," his mother said. "And perhaps we might refurbish the nursery. Yes, a trip to Bath would be of utmost importance. Frilled curtains at the windows, a new table and set of chairs, a new canopy for her bed. Oh, there is so much to do." She looked elated at the prospect.

"Mother, I wondered if we might bring Miranda with us, as well, to help with Ellie," Gerard said.

Some of the annoyance crept back into her face. "Whyever would we do that?"

"Ellie has become very attached to Miranda, and she could serve as Ellie's nursery maid."

"Ellie will soon become attached to *me*," his mother

said. "And we could hire a nursery maid from the village."

He should not have mentioned Ellie's attachment, for it was making his mother defensive and possessive. "It is only for a few weeks or a few months at most."

"All the more reason for her not to stay with us," she said. "Ellie will only miss Miranda the more when she leaves."

"My dear, we only are thinking of your own comfort," his father said.

"You needn't be concerned about me," his mother replied. "And I must say, John, that I am rather surprised that you would agree with Gerard in this. A penniless young woman, not related by blood, under our roof? It would be most improper."

Heat crawled up Gerard's neck and jaw. "I am in no danger from Miranda. We know each other too well."

"You are not alleviating my concern," she said.

"I don't think Miranda has a heart to be captured by any man," Gerard said. "She is still as quiet and self-controlled as ever she was as a child."

"Your mother is correct, Gerard," his father said. "A young woman under our roof ..."

"If you are ill at ease, I will move to Foremont Lacy." He had not seen his property, inherited from his grandmother, since he had come ashore. "I will soon be well enough that I can do with only a manservant."

"But that is only ..." His mother checked herself. "I am still unconvinced that it is necessary to bring Miranda with us."

Gerard had not considered his marital prospects since becoming injured, but he now realized that nothing had prevented his mother from thinking of such things, especially now that he was living in his father's house. And apparently, in his mother's opinion, his residence at the neighboring farm of Foremont Lacy would still be too uncomfortably close to Foremont Court, should Miranda take up residence there.

His father's look convinced Gerard to abandon the subject. "I would not distress you, madam."

"Yes, your convalescence has been quite distressing enough," she said peevishly.

He was rescued by the appearance of their evening tea, which also included an ornate silver punch bowl of wassail. However, on his way to get a cup of the Christmas drink, he was waylaid by Miss Church-Pratton, one of Felicity's cousins.

"Now why were you men sequestered together for so long?" She gave a trilling laugh. "I had begun to fear you had abandoned us."

"Business, I fear," Gerard said politely.

"Oh, you mustn't work during Christmastide." She smiled, and dimples appeared in her cheeks. "Is not the company amusing enough?"

"Indeed." She had been seated next to him at the dinner table, and while she spent a few scant minutes talking to her partner on her other side, she spent the rest of the time talking to him. About herself.

Even aside from that, Gerard was mistrustful of her smiles. He'd heard from Lady Wynwood, who obviously disliked Miss Church-Pratton, that she had broken her engagement earlier this year to an officer who had been wounded at Corunna. However, the Season in London had not resulted in a second engagement, and Gerard could see that her charm had an edge of bitterness and desperation.

He had no intention of being her next matrimonial target. With his injury, he was in no condition to even consider a more distant future with any woman. He must concentrate on the most immediate needs, namely being able to discard his cane and to relieve the burden upon his parents.

It was a cowardly thing to do, but he simply grasped at the first idea that came to mind. He took a small glass of wassail from the maid serving the punch at a side table and then wobbled on his cane, spilling the drink on his waistcoat. The scent of wine, nutmeg, and apples grew stronger, and he felt the warmth as the hot beverage soaked through his shirt.

"Oh, dear!" Miss Church-Pratton fished out her handkerchief, a thin lawn square the size of a playing card, and swabbed at his chest.

Her hand seemed to be touching a larger area of his chest than the spill, and he hastily stepped away from her suspicious ministrations. "I do beg your pardon, Miss Church-Pratton. I must change my waistcoat before it stains." He turned and left.

He thumped his way down the hallway. His bedroom was smaller than the bedrooms in the other wings, but it was close to the drawing room, just past the library and the ballroom. The carpet runner narrowed here, and he stumbled when the tip of his cane slid a few inches because it had touched down on the polished wooden floor rather than the rug.

He and his father were sharing a valet during the visit so that Cecil would not need to house an extra servant in his bursting household, but Gerard did not bother to call Maddox to assist him. His evening wear hung loosely on his frame since his return home, and he had become used to dressing himself while on board ship. He easily shrugged out of his coat, waistcoat, and shirt, although the clean shirt he pulled on was not quite as creaseless as Maddox would have wanted. Gerard pulled out the first waistcoat he saw, which was striped in gray and blue and perhaps more suited to morning wear, but the cravat he tied was unexceptionable, if not overly elaborate.

He made his way out of his room, but he could faintly hear a woman's voice, shrill with displeasure. At first it sounded like Miss Church-Pratton, but then he realized it was Felicity. A low man's voice answered her—Cecil. The voices came from the library door, opened a crack, and it was obvious they were arguing.

"Things take her twice as long as anyone else," Felicity said. "Or she does something completely ridiculous. Last week, the governess was ill so she was supposed to take over Ellie's instruction. Instead, she took her skating on the pond. She said it was to teach her mathematics!"

He couldn't be certain, but he thought they might be speaking of Miranda. She had always had an unconventional way of thinking of the world, which had made her a delightful playmate when they were children. She was also the type of person who was patient, no matter what the task.

The library was far enough from the drawing room that no one there would hear them, but Gerard's room was closer. He began thumping along as quickly as possible, hoping neither of the angry couple would suddenly storm out of the library and see him skulking like a thief. The distance to the drawing room seemed like a mile.

"She's impossible," Felicity hissed. "She does it on purpose to upset me."

"I hardly think she does it on purpose," Cecil said. "She's always been like that, a bit touched in the head."

"Well then, I don't want a madwoman in my home. I shall be heartily glad when she goes to my cousin Polly's house."

Gerard moved to the far side of the hallway as he passed the library door. Calling Miranda a madwoman was a bit much, even for Felicity's spiteful nature. Miranda had always been unique, uncaring of what others thought of her, comfortable in who she was and unapologetic about it. But perhaps in Felicity's mind, the fact that Miranda wouldn't scurry to obey her every command would seem like the actions of a madwoman.

Suddenly his cane again landed on the wooden floor, a good foot of which lay between the edge of the carpet runner and the wall. This time, the tip slid quickly. His knee twisted at the sudden loss of support. A sharp pain sliced up his leg. He didn't feel the impact as he hit the floor, just saw the carpet runner rise up to meet him. As he lay there, he panted heavily and screwed his eyes shut, focusing on pushing past the pain in his knee so he wouldn't faint. He could smell dust, mold, and the faintest hint of lemon polish.

He didn't realize he had blocked out all sound until Cecil's voice broke into the haze of pain.

"As to that, Mr. Foremont wanted her to go with

Ellie, to help out for a few months."

Gerard had to get out of this hallway. He couldn't bear it if someone came along and saw him on the floor, or worse, if Cecil and Felicity left the library and realized he had fallen nearly across the threshold. He pushed at the floor, rising on his good knee. His entire leg was shaking.

"Absolutely not," Felicity said. "Polly didn't come this year because her youngest broke his leg and they lost yet another nursery maid. She needs Miranda."

"What your cousin needs is to learn how to keep her maids from quitting her service."

"It is the best solution for us to loan Miranda to Polly. Miranda cannot quit service."

Gerard got to his feet and leaned against the wall for a moment, catching his breath. His heart pounded as if he'd run up ten flights of stairs. He continued toward the drawing room at a slower pace, his knee aching with each step.

But even more than the pain in his leg, he felt the burning of injustice and frustration in his gut. Miranda was little better than a slave in this household. He could not bear to see her so abused.

His only goal had been to become well in body, but oughtn't he to exercise his conscience, as well? How could he stand to allow Cecil and Felicity to treat her so? Surely he could do more to convince his mother to change her mind.

There had been so many men, so many friends he had not been able to save during the war. Now that he was ashore, at the very least he could save one childhood friend.

Chapter Four

December 24th

The morning had dawned crisp and cold, but clear enough for the annual Christmas greens collecting. Laura, Lady Wynwood, finished tying the scarf about Sally's neck. The little girl had grown so much since Laura had seen her last Christmas here at Wintrell Hall. "There, now you are ready to gather mistletoe."

"William says mistletoe is for grown-ups."

"And who is William?"

"He is the rector's son. Back at home in Sussex."

Laura smiled and smoothed the brown curls peeking out from beneath the girl's hood. "Mistletoe is for the kissing bough, so I suppose he's right, after a fashion."

Sally made a face. "Why do grown-ups like kissing so much? William said that sometimes when grown-ups kiss, they make babies."

Laura choked back a laugh. "No, they most certainly do not make babies simply from kissing. But grown-ups do enjoy it."

Sally gave her a suspicious look. "Do you enjoy

kissing?"

"I enjoy kissing you." Laura grabbed her in a hug and rained kisses upon her round cheeks.

Sally squealed and giggled. "Now you must kiss Paul," she told Laura.

Sally's cousin, who had been pulling on his mittens nearby, scowled and backed up a few steps. "I'm too old for kissing. Kissing is for babies."

"I'm not a baby."

"You're the baby cousin. There isn't anyone younger than you."

Sally turned to Laura. "Cousin Laura, you should have babies so that I will no longer be the youngest."

It surprised Laura that the innocent remark caused such a sharp pang in her heart, even after all these years. She imagined she could feel an answering pain in her stomach. She gave Sally a bright smile. "Babies require a papa, and I have no husband."

"You should marry Mr. Drydale."

"No, Mr. Drydale and I are friends. Like you and William, the rector's son. Now off with you." She gave Sally a little push out the front door as the other cousins also filed outside.

No, Sol deserved better than someone like her. She was not being self-pitying, but practical. He needed a woman who could bear him an heir, and she would not put herself under the control of a man. Never again.

Laura secured her own hood and followed the troupe of children. They all headed across the lawn in front of the house toward the edge of the forest. A pale winter sun squinted through the hazy clouds, turning the grass a sage-green color. Her breath blew around her head, and when she inhaled, she smelled woodsmoke.

She was watching Paul chase Sally in circles around the lawn when she became aware of someone who had come to walk beside her. "Good morning, Miranda."

"Good morning, Cousin Laura."

"Where is Ellie?" It had been obvious that Ellie clung to Miranda like a barnacle on a ship, and no wonder—the child had lost her mother less than a year ago, and then been thrust into Cecil's cold household. And Miranda was the sort of person you could cling to, who wouldn't mind you doing it.

"Ellie is there." Miranda pointed to a small figure walking with Augusta's youngest daughter, who was fifteen. "Liliana has promised to make snow angels with her if they find a patch of snow."

"Snow? Not yet, I fear."

"Ellie is still hopeful." Miranda smiled, and it transformed her face from plain to pixie-like. But the smile was fleeting, and as it faded, lines appeared on the sides of her mouth. "Cousin Laura, I have a favor to ask. But I should like it if you did not tell Cecil about it."

Laura raised her eyebrows. "Cecil?"

Miranda's cheeks turned rosy, but Laura did not believe it was from the biting winter wind. "I have already spoken briefly with Aunt Augusta, and she was quite distressed at my request. I should not wish to upset Cecil."

"Of course. I will not speak to him about our private conversation."

"Thank you." Miranda's exhaled breath hung like a cloud about her head. "Cousin Laura, you have a great many friends and relations. Do you know of any ladies who might need a paid companion?"

Laura was not surprised by the question. While she knew very little about Miranda's situation, she had noticed that Felicity treated Miranda with less respect than her relationship as Cecil's cousin deserved. However, it was not uncommon for poor relations to be treated like servants—she had seen it in other households, with women even more arrogant than Felicity Belmoore.

And yet Miranda's face never betrayed any discomfort. She had always kept her feelings to herself.

"Of course. I shall write to my friends directly," Laura said.

"Thank you. If you do hear of a position, please write to me at the home of Felicity's cousin, Polly Beatty, outside of Weymouth."

A chill raced up Laura's spine, and it was not from the winter wind. But perhaps she was mistaken. "I did not know you were close to Felicity's cousin," she said lightly. "How long will you be visiting?"

There was an awkward pause. "I will not be visiting. After Twelfth Night, Felicity is sending me to help as their nursery maid."

Laura stopped walking and grasped Miranda's elbow. "She cannot hire her own nursery maid? Or beg the help of one of her relations?"

Miranda would not look at Laura. "She has difficulty retaining her servants."

Laura knew why, although she was not certain if Miranda did, also. Laura had no wish to frighten her, but she could not allow her to walk into that house without warning. "You cannot go," Laura croaked.

Miranda's cheeks had become as gray as the sky. She hesitated, then whispered, "Are the rumors true?"

"Oh, my dear girl. I must tell Felicity—"

"She did not believe me."

Of course Felicity would not, that wretched, selfish woman.

Laura had never known Miranda well because her father had not been one of Laura's favorite cousins. Charles Belmoore had been a scowl on two legs, and his wife had had the perpetual expression of someone smelling fish gone bad.

But she could not allow Felicity to do this to Miranda. Laura had been forced to endure her horrific marriage to her late husband, but it had given her the means and independence to do what was right.

"If only I could take you home with me," Laura said. "But I am promised to my aunt in Northumbria after Twelfth Night, and my townhouse in London is being renovated while I am away. Perhaps I may write to my aunt ..."

"Lady Wynwood, Miranda," said a strong male voice, "good morning to you both."

Laura would normally welcome Gerard's company, had Miranda's plight not been so troubling. Because of Mr. Foremont's close friendship with Laura's cousin Edward, she had known Gerard since he was in leading strings. She was surprised to see the grave lines in his forehead as he looked at Miranda.

However, he turned to her with a smile. "It is good to see you, my lady. I had not time for more than a quick hello last evening."

"You are looking remarkably well." He was, for

although he walked slowly and carefully with his cane on the wet, brittle grass, it was a marked improvement from only a month ago when she had seen him briefly in London. He had been in town with his parents to visit his doctor, and he had been using crutches rather than a cane.

"Thank you." He glanced away briefly, and she thought she saw the same bitter frustration behind his eyes that she'd seen a month ago.

Perhaps he was not as improved as she had thought.

"My father and I have spoken to Cecil and Mr. Belmoore," Gerard said. "It is decided that Ellie is to come home with us."

"That's wonderful," Laura said.

"I must thank you again for your suggestion to my mother. The anticipation of having Ellie in her care has made her quite cheerful." His eyes slid to Miranda, then he said to Laura, "I wish to beg another favor from you, my lady. Would you perhaps exert your influence over my mother to allow Miranda to accompany Ellie to Foremont Court for a few months?"

Laura gasped. "That is a very good idea."

He blinked. "It is? Er ... that is, just so."

Miranda was looking at him with surprise. "Gerard, your mother ..."

"We have nearly a fortnight to convince her," he said, more to Miranda than to Laura. "I am certain that with Lady Wynwood's help, we may do so."

"Of course I will help you," Laura said. She could think of no better way to prevent Miranda from being sent to the Beattys.

Color had returned to Miranda's cheeks. "Would you,

Cousin Laura?"

"My dear." Laura stopped to take Miranda's hands in hers. "Of course I will. And it will only be for a few weeks, perhaps a few months. After I help my aunt organize the repair of her cottage, I insist that you come to stay with me in my townhouse in London."

"Do you need a companion?"

"Not particularly," Laura said cheerfully, "and I suspect you would be a poor one. You do not scurry nervously. And I have seen your embroidery—it is atrocious, so you would not be able to untangle your employer's silks."

A smile tugged at Miranda's lips.

"If you will be able to stay with the Foremonts until I come to retrieve you, then you will join me in London as my guest. You may stay as long as you like, or I can find a position for you if you desire it. I only regret I cannot have you with me immediately, but my aunt's cottage has only one useable bedroom. In fact, I shall be sleeping on the sofa for part of the time, and there is no inn within a comfortable distance."

Miranda squeezed Laura's hands tightly, but the girl said nothing, her eyes large and luminous.

"You quite exhaust me with your exuberance," Laura said.

"I am confident we shall prevail, Miranda," Gerard said. "You will be happy at Foremont Court before long."

It was just a flicker of a glance that Miranda sent to Gerard before she looked away, but the certainty struck Laura like a blow. Miranda was in love with Gerard. It might be a girlhood infatuation, but the feelings were there, waiting to mature into true, deep affection.

Laura was no matchmaker, but a part of her wished for happiness for Miranda and Gerard, each of whom was lonely in their own way. She must convince Mary Foremont to allow Miranda to travel back to their home with them and with Ellie, but would she only be encouraging a situation that would result in heartbreak for Miranda?

Or would two hearts somehow find each other across the gulf of Miranda's protective shell and Gerard's bitterness?

Chapter Five

Miranda welcomed the distraction of picking Christmas greens to decorate the house. Everyone was in a merry mood, no one paying attention to her, and she could calm herself.

She had thought Gerard would not expend much effort for her request to his mother, and had expected that path to be closed to her. His actions in enlisting the help of Cousin Laura had not only surprised her, but had caused hope to blossom in her chest.

She ought not to hope. It always led to disappointment.

And yet what else could she do when two people were suddenly championing her? She was unaccustomed to such consideration, for her parents' treatment of her had taught her to avoid depending upon others.

Therefore, it had been particularly difficult for her to ask Aunt Augusta for help, only to be accused of ingratitude for Cecil's benevolence. After such criticism, Miranda had nearly not approached Laura with the same request. But then Laura had been so concerned, and Gerard had surprised her with his persistence in helping her.

Would they succeed in convincing his mother? And yet, she was afraid to hope.

She took a deep breath, letting the quiet of the forest soothe her. The trees had the feel of age and patience, perseverance through storms and overzealous woodchoppers. She imagined she could hear the trees whispering to each other even now, rustling in arboreal gossip over the excited chatter of women and children gathering greenery.

How the paths of her life had shifted only a scant hour or two ago. Everything seemed too wonderful to possibly be more than a dream that would melt away—staying with Ellie and the Foremonts, and then with Cousin Laura. Escaping the Beattys. No longer needing to withstand Felicity's impatience and determination to put Miranda in her proper place as a humble, grateful dependent.

Would her circumstances truly be different after Twelfth Night? It was hard to imagine how they would be, because she had felt for a long time that she was slowly disappearing, like a ghost fading away into mist. She didn't know if she could be happy. She couldn't remember the last time she had been.

"'Randa." Ellie broke into her thoughts. She had been following Miranda and holding the fir boughs that she cut.

"Yes, darling?"

"Paul said he will get the biggest branch."

"Oh, did he? We shall see if we can best him."

Ellie grinned, and it was Miranda's cousin Edmund who smiled at her in the shape of her mouth, the crinkling of her eyes. But she had her mother's blue eyes and golden-brown hair, fine as silk.

Miranda had done this every Christmas Eve with her Belmoore relatives—the women and children picking mistletoe, ivy, and fir boughs while the men and farmhands went out to collect the massive Yule log, which would burn in the oversized medieval fireplace in the great entry hall until the end of Twelfth Night.

Gerard came up beside her, but spoke to Ellie, whose arms were so full of fir boughs that they trailed down behind her. "Take care, Ellie, or you will trip over your green dress."

She looked at the dripping fir, then giggled and twirled in a circle, making the branches fly out around her, and a few flung off through the undergrowth.

"You'll lose everything we've collected," Miranda said with a smile.

"I'll go get them. Come, Ellie." Gerard went off the path, making a dramatic effort as he swung his cane at the scraggly bushes, pretending to get lost as he searched for the missing firs.

The last time Miranda had gathered greenery with Gerard had been sixteen years ago, the Christmas before he went to sea. He would have been with the men and the Yule log if his knee had allowed him to keep up or allowed him to ride a horse without pain. He joked with Ellie and with the other children, but every so often, the distant sound of a man's voice in the woods made him look up, and a harshness would settle over his face like a mask.

Or perhaps his cheerfulness was the mask.

She admitted that some of the fear—no, probably

most of the fear she felt was how, if she went to the Foremonts' home, she would be so close to Gerard for the first time in years. Yes, fear that she wouldn't be able to hide her feelings from him, or even worse, from his parents.

She was used to hiding. She'd had to hide who she was, it seemed, all her life—from her own parents, from most of her family. People seemed to constantly remind her that she could never be quite the same as the rest of society. That she was different.

Her father had been disappointed that she wasn't charming, that she was too quiet and uninteresting. Her mother had been upset that she'd been hopeless at catching a husband during her Season. Felicity disliked her so much that she was eager to foist her off rather than keeping an unpaid servant.

And aside from all that, there was the one secret no one could know, the one sin she could never rub out.

She had no wish to open herself to anyone, and certainly not handsome, confident Gerard. He would find her lacking, as so many other people in her life had done, and if she loved him, his disappointment or rejection would flay her alive.

So she had to somehow crush her feelings for him. Burn them out of her heart.

Not all the trees had lost their leaves, and combined with the fitful winter sun, the dimness made it seem even colder. Gerard and Ellie had wandered away from Miranda, and she determined to keep herself apart from him. Ellie needed to become used to Gerard, who was a stranger to her.

Miranda tramped through the undergrowth,

distancing herself from the other women and children, deeper into the silence and darkness of the forest. Even their voices became muffled by the tree trunks and low-hanging branches.

Behind her, leaves rustled, then a stick snapped. And then something heavy collided with the base of her neck.

Pain exploded throughout her skull. She didn't remember falling to the ground, but she became aware of dead leaves under her cheek, the overpowering scent of mildew and dirt. Her limbs felt chained to the ground.

Something blocked the dim light, and she saw the edge of a dark cloak dragging in the wet leaves. Hands ran over her body as though searching for something. She tried to roll over, but the attacker was leaning hard against her back.

Then she felt, through the ground, the heavier tread of boots, the lighter touch of a cane. No. She had to warn Gerard. He had Ellie with him.

The steps stopped. "Miranda!" he shouted.

The hands touching her froze.

He hastened toward her at the same time her attacker moved away. Miranda rolled over.

There was a blur, a swirl of skirts, and then a heavy branch swung through the air at Gerard's head. He ducked, but the action made him stagger against his cane.

"Gerard!" she gasped. Miranda was behind the attacker and saw nothing but a dark cloak.

Then she saw Ellie standing a few feet away from Gerard. The girl had frozen, her face aghast. Fir boughs slowly rained down upon the ground.

Gerard's expression looked more shocked than injured.

But then the woman swung the branch again and hit his hip. He grimaced and fell to his knee, losing his cane.

But this time, the branch clipped Ellie on the head, and the little girl crumpled.

"Ellie!" Strength surged through her, and Miranda scrabbled through the leaves and bushes on her hands and knees.

The woman aimed a third blow at Gerard's head, but he was able to grab the branch in both hands. The two of them struggled.

It seemed an age before Miranda reached Ellie's form on the ground. The little girl was screaming. She gathered her into her arms and tried to drag her away from Gerard and the woman, turning her back to them to protect Ellie.

Grunting, frantic movements in the undergrowth. Then the woman cried out, her voice sounding as if she were being flung away.

Miranda turned her head to look and saw a heap of wool fabric several feet away from Gerard. He had taken the heavy branch the woman had used. He tried to rise to his feet, but his knee buckled and he fell again.

The woman scrambled up and darted away into the trees.

"Stop!" he shouted. Miranda heard the razor edge of frustration in his voice as he rose unsteadily, leaning for support on the branch that he still held.

Miranda used her scarf to dab at Ellie's forehead, which was smeared with blood. The branch had cut her, but it did not appear to be deep, and Ellie's cries were wrenching sobs of terror rather than pain.

Gerard retrieved his cane and hobbled toward them.

"Who was that?"

"I don't know," Miranda said.

"Did you see her face?"

"No."

"Are you injured? Is Ellie hurt?"

At that moment, Cousin Laura ran toward them. "What happened? Good gracious, is that blood?"

Aunt Augusta followed close behind with some of the other children. "What happened?"

"A woman attacked Miranda," Gerard said. "When I came upon her, she appeared to be looking for valuables in Miranda's cloak. When I tried to stop her, the woman accidentally hit Ellie."

"Poor dear." Cousin Laura drew near, but Ellie buried her face deeper into Miranda's shoulder, her crying muffled.

"Let us take the children back to the house," Laura said. "We should have enough greenery by now. Who would attack you?"

"Was it a Gypsy?" Aunt Augusta asked. "I hadn't heard of any Gypsies in the area."

"I don't know." Miranda started to shake her head, but the movement made pain cloud her vision.

"Miranda, you're injured," Gerard said.

"I am well. We must take Ellie away from here."

They all turned back toward the house. Cousin Laura and Miranda's aunts counted children and went to collect any stragglers while Miranda carried Ellie tightly against her.

Gerard was walking more slowly, leaning more heavily on his cane. She watched him, and had a drowning feeling in her lungs. Suddenly her plan to somehow erase her feelings for him no longer seemed so simple.

When the woman attacked him, and she'd seen Gerard go down, she'd known deep in her heart that she couldn't bear to lose him.

Chapter Six

Gerard pulled his mouth wide in what he hoped looked like a smile and passed Miss Church-Pratton a fir branch.

"Oh, Captain Foremont, are you certain your leg is not paining you?" She gave him a soulful look that brought out the blue of her eyes.

"I am perfectly well, Miss Church-Pratton." Gerard ignored the ache in his knee.

"I do appreciate your help but I would not wish to cause you further injury."

He tried to stretch his leg without drawing attention to the action. He seemed to be mostly recovered from the events of this morning in the woods. He moved a little more slowly and he could not climb the ladder to decorate the chandelier, but he was perfectly able to collect greenery and deliver it to the women who arranged it around the house. Unfortunately, Miss Church-Pratton seemed to call upon him quite incessantly for more greens.

"For I must tell you, Captain Foremont," Miss Church-Pratton said as she wrapped ribbon around a fir bough and strand of ivy, "I was alarmed when I saw you limping so dreadfully as you came into the house."

He would rather not be reminded of that riotous scene, complete with schoolboys chasing each other around the entrance hall, yelling at the tops of their lungs, and Mrs. Augusta Hathaway shrieking about Gypsies attacking children in the woods. Ellie's cries had turned to sniffles by the time they arrived at the house, but the noise had caused her to start crying again. Gerard had tried to speak to Miranda but hadn't been able to get close to her.

"It must have been terrible for you."

Miss Church-Pratton's fussing over Gerard annoyed him, but he tried to tell himself that she was simply concerned.

"Now, if I had known you would be going greenery hunting rather than with the men hauling in the Yule log, I would have gone with all of you," Miss Church-Pratton said.

Gerard had been secretly relieved that she had not joined the greenery party this morning. He had suspected that she had no wish to be in the company of all the children.

"Perhaps I could have protected you from that madwoman." She smiled, dimpling up at him.

Considering the horrible violence that Ellie had been forced to witness, Gerard found Miss Church-Pratton's comment inappropriate. He looked down at her coldly. "You no longer appear to need assistance, Miss Church-Pratton. I shall help my mother." He gave her the tiniest of bows, then crossed the room to where his mother was directing a servant on a ladder in hanging the kissing bough directly over the open doorway into the drawing room.

His mother eyed the expression on his face with wariness and a splash of irritation. "I do wish you would stop focusing on your injury quite so much, Gerard. You may not be aware of it, but it casts a pall over the company, which is not very considerate of you."

He did not feel he deserved his mother's censure, but she had seen him through the blackest of moods over the past several months, and he knew it had put a strain on her temper. And the truth was that he did indeed feel frustrated with himself, not a novel emotion by any means. He had not been able to chase the lone woman because he had been unable to rise quickly to his feet, and he would not have been able to hobble after her in any event.

Added to his frustration was a strong dose of guilt. He had been horrified that Ellie had been injured simply because she had been standing too close when the woman had swung the branch at him.

"No, to the right," his mother said to the servant, who obediently moved the kissing bough to his right. "No, the other right." She indicated her own right side. "Miranda, is it centered?"

Miranda had been tying greens into a long garland to drape over the banister, but she rose to stand in front of the open doorway, her head tilted to the side. "Perhaps a little to the right ..."

Miranda appeared to be her usual calm self, although paler. A half hour after returning to the house, Gerard had climbed the stairs to see Ellie in the nursery, and Miranda had been there after finally coaxing the little girl to sleep. Miranda had not looked as though her nerves were frayed or that she was likely to take to her bed, which was what Gerard's mother had done for an hour after he returned. Miranda had insisted that the blow to her head had merely caused her a slight headache.

She had changed her dress, as had they all, for dinner. Her dark blue gown made her skin even whiter, her hair glossy like a raven's feathers. When he first saw her, she looked so lovely that he hadn't been able to speak for a moment. Luckily, she hadn't been looking at him, and then all the guests had begun the task of decorating the house with the greenery.

"Are you well?" he asked her.

"A slight headache."

He could see the pain in the lines across her forehead, alongside her mouth and eyes. He would have wanted to look at the base of her neck, hidden by the folds of her shawl, if it had not been so improper for him to do so. "Has the apothecary seen you?"

"No, but one of the maids has seen to my injury."

"One of the maids? Cecil did not call for Dr. Morgan for you or for Ellie?"

"Betty, the maid, is very skilled in healing," she said in a calm voice that alleviated his outrage. "Her mother is the local midwife, and the tenants call upon her when they cannot summon Dr. Morgan. I admit that I would trust Betty more than Dr. Morgan, since he often comes to the house smelling of wine."

He determined not to summon Dr. Morgan if his knee grew worse, and to do all he could to prevent the man from coming near Miranda or Ellie. "How is Ellie?"

"She woke several hours ago, and while she is quieter than usual, she seems to be well. I left her playing jack straws with her cousins."

"I am glad." He had never felt so alarmed as when he had looked at Ellie and seen blood on her face. Although the sight of Miranda on the ground had made his heart stop in his chest.

"No, to the *other* right," his mother told the servant.

"The kissing bough looks nice," Gerard said, immediately regretting how inane that sounded. Earlier, Felicity had grown impatient with Miranda because she was not draping the greenery in the dining room as quickly as she wished, and so she had assigned to her the task of creating the kissing bough. Miranda had twined the mistletoe upon the wire frames with scarlet ribbons and roses made from twisted red paper. Stars cut from gold paper peeked out from under the dark green leaves and pearly white berries.

"Thank you," Miranda said. Miss Church-Pratton would have laughed and teased him, but Miranda accepted his words without judgment on how foolish he sounded. "Your knee is paining you?" She stated it calmly, already knowing the answer.

"No, I am—"

"There is a poultice I can make for you that will soothe it. I shall give it to your man later."

He wanted to say that he was well and in no need of any poultices, but Miranda was known for her skill in the stillroom. If it would indeed ease the pain, he ought not to indulge his pride and act like a muttonhead. *Say thank you, Gerard.* "Er ... thank you, Miranda."

"You are welcome."

No fussing. No censure. Just a poultice for his knee. Miranda put him at ease like no one else had cared to do.

He caught his mother looking at them both, but the expression on her face was difficult to interpret. Some alarm—Gerard had not forgotten the embarrassing insinuation that Miranda would attempt to ensnare him just as Miss Church-Pratton seemed to be doing—but also some confusion, perhaps a thread of guilt. No, he must be mistaken about that. His mother looked away again.

"Why would that woman attack you when there were so many people nearby?" he asked.

"I had wandered away from all of you," she said.

"We were fortunate that Ellie had lost sight of you and become alarmed. I went to look for you, and none too soon."

"It is also fortunate that I had nothing for her to steal."

"Now it is time to test it." It was his father, just come into the drawing room and admiring the kissing bough, which the servant had finally hung to his mother's specifications.

His father snatched his mother's hand and yanked her under the kissing bough. She gave a surprised yelp, then a delighted gurgle. He kissed her firmly on the lips, then reached up to remove one of the berries. When all the berries were gone, there would be no more stolen kisses.

Cecil looked scandalized but resigned, for there had always been a kissing bough at Wintrell Hall for as long as the Belmoores had celebrated Christmas there.

"It's almost time!" came a call from outside the

drawing room. They all trooped to the doorway to the dining room, where Cecil held a large wax candle that had been decorated with gilt paper round its base.

Children came down the stairs to gather with the adults, and Cecil looked with pride at the assembly. He did enjoy theatrics when it made him look important.

"It is sunset, and now we will light the Yule candle," he intoned. He led the way into the dining room, which had been magnificently decorated and set for the Christmas Eve feast. To accommodate all the guests, including the children, chairs had been shoved close to each other around the long table.

The guests stopped at the door while Cecil bore the candle to a special glass candle holder in the center of the table. A servant approached with a lit taper, and with great solemnity, Cecil lit the candle.

"Happy Christmas," he said, as though at a funeral.

In contrast, everyone responded with a rousing, "Happy Christmas!"

"May we be blessed by the light of the Yule candle," Cecil said.

It did indeed look beautiful on the table. It was large enough that it would burn until dawn Christmas morning. Cecil would extinguish the flame just before the entire household left for church.

Everyone filed around the table with many smiles and appreciative sniffs at the feast to come. They all stood behind their chairs, waiting for everyone to find their places, and then at Cecil's signal, they all sat at table at the same time. It had always been so. As a child, Gerard had been told it was to prevent bad luck.

He again found himself seated next to Miss Church-

Pratton. Everyone was squeezed rather tightly together, but she seemed to rub her arm against his shoulder much more than Liliana, one of Mrs. Hathaway's daughters still in the schoolroom, on his other side.

The meal was generous, with roast goose, boar's head, venison, chicken, and turkey. There were more vegetable dishes than he could see from his seat, including potatoes, parsnips, Brussels sprouts, and carrots, as well as stuffing. The meal tomorrow night would be even more lavish.

Also according to tradition, everyone rose from the table at the same time. No after-dinner port and cigars for the gentlemen—everyone gathered in the drawing room. The tension of anticipation filled the room as the servants doused the candles, and then came a moment of breathless silence.

The doors opened and the butler entered with a mound of raisins in a large shallow bowl. A footman lit a taper from the fire and set the brandy-soaked fruit ablaze.

Oooh rose from the children as the blue flame blazed in the darkness, turning the butler's staid face rather sinister. As he placed the bowl upon a low table in the center of the room, it was the adults who led the traditional song:

Here comes the flaming bowl,
Don't he mean to take his toll,
Snip! Snap! Dragon!
Take care you don't take too much,
Be not greedy in your clutch,
Snip! Snap! Dragon!

Then adults and children alike gathered 'round for a game of Snapdragon, with each person reaching in to snatch a flaming raisin and eat it without being burned. Servants hovered nearby, ready to douse any inadvertent fires set by dropped raisins.

In the darkness, Gerard contrived to sneak away from Miss Church-Pratton and move about the dark room, straining to see each of the people in shadow. Then he saw Miranda, seated by the window with a bundle in her arms. As he approached, he saw that Ellie was asleep on her lap.

"You will not allow her to play Snapdragon?" he asked.

"Most certainly not," she retorted.

"I seem to recall that we played at a fairly young age."

"And at that tender age, you burned both your sleeve and your eyebrows, do you recall?"

He laughed. "I had forgotten."

She looked at the blue light in the center of the room, which flickered as people moved in front of it. "I like the light. It is mysterious and lovely. But I admit I like it better from a distance." She turned her face toward him, and even in the darkness he could see the gleam of her smile.

He answered with one of his own, and he reached out to touch her cheek because it seemed the most natural and necessary thing for him to do. As in the carriage when he had touched her hand, he wanted to be connected to her in a powerful way that he could not understand.

Her skin trembled beneath his fingers, and then she turned her face away.

He suddenly felt awkward and large. He clasped his hands in front of him on his cane, then tucked one hand behind him, then he shifted his feet, except that he put too much weight on his injured knee. He winced.

"Does it hurt you?" she asked.

He didn't know how she could have known, in the dark. "It is stiff."

"I shall send the poultice to you after I put Ellie to bed." She made as if to rise, but he remembered why he had sought her out.

"Stay. I have a question to ask you." He didn't need to, but he put a hand on her shoulder—again, that desire to touch her. He left it there for a moment, even after she had settled back into the chair, Ellie still fast asleep in her arms.

"Have you thought more about the woman?"

"Yes." As usual, she surprised him. "I have wondered if perhaps the attack was not by chance. But ..."

When she did not continue, he said, "You are very insightful. I should like to hear your thoughts. Can you think of anyone who would wish to harm you?"

She hesitated longer than he would have expected, but then said, "No. I have no family and no fortune. I had one Season in London and have spent the rest of my life in the country, first with my parents and then with Cecil."

"But we cannot dismiss the possibility simply because we cannot think of a good motivation. You must be careful."

She looked up at him again, and although he couldn't see her eyes, something made him feel rather fevered. He added, "After all, Ellie is often with you. I am concerned for both of you, of course. It was only by chance that she was nearer to me in the forest, and that you were farther away from the rest of the party."

"Of course." Her voice sounded hollow. She rose to her feet, carrying Ellie. "If you will excuse me, I must be awake early to help Felicity with the preparations for the ball tomorrow." The Christmas Day ball had been a tradition at Wintrell Hall much like the kissing bough.

He didn't want her to leave him. "It sounds as though Felicity has invited all the county."

"There are more guests this year than last year. We have hired twice the usual number of local people to help tomorrow." She suddenly stiffened.

"What is it?" He moved closer to her.

Miranda turned, and they stood close to one another, face to face, Ellie's sleeping form between them. He could smell lavender and lemon, soothing and yet also tart, like her.

"The villagers all know me," she said in a low voice. "None of them would have attacked me because they all know I am a poor relation and have nothing of value. So it must have been someone newly come to the village."

"I could make inquiries, determine whether anyone has arrived recently."

"They will hardly speak to you, especially if it is someone who knows the woman who attacked me. Can you send your valet?"

"I am sharing my father's man, and the local residents know him well because of my father's longtime friendship with Mr. Belmoore."

"Is there another servant? A stranger? Someone the woman would not know is connected to the Belmoores."

"There is no other servant here with us who would be suitable, but ..." He suddenly knew who he could use. "I will think of something."

She smiled calmly, not needling him for more information or pouting that he would not confide in her. "Good night, Gerard."

"Good night, Miranda."

He watched her leave, still carrying Ellie, and then he left the drawing room through another door. He knocked on the door to the library, then opened it to an empty room.

Seating himself at Cecil's desk, he took out a quill and paper and proceeded to write.

Chapter Seven

December 25th

"You look pretty," Ellie said to Miranda.

"Thank you." She stood in front of the small mirror on the wall of Miss Teel's room, pinning her dark hair. She had made several narrow braids and coiled them in a simple pattern that looked like a more complex one, at first glance.

Miss Teel had already dressed and was helping some of the older schoolgirls with their toilettes, since the entire family were to dine together again tonight before the ball. Miranda normally took very little heed of her own dress, but tonight she wanted to look ... different. Even though she knew there was no reason for it.

Not that she had much choice in what to wear. When she had been living with her parents, they had attended parties and dances, but Miranda had not always accompanied them—the crowded rooms made her feel as though she couldn't breathe, and her conversation became even more insipid than usual. So her wardrobe even then had been small. Now, she had but two evening gowns, the dark blue one she had worn last night and this one.

It was her favorite. She had altered it herself from a gown her mother had no longer wanted, a pale green silk with the fuller cut that had recently fallen out of fashion. Miranda had trimmed it with emerald green ribbon, and then embroidered the fabric in a delicate pattern of gold leaves, which had taken a painstakingly long time because her embroidery was, in general, rather poor. It was old, and it did not fit her quite as well as she would have liked, but she was pleased at how her mediocre embroidery had fared and took pleasure in the feminine way the skirt swished about her ankles.

"I must take this from you now, you scamp." She removed the necklace from around Ellie's neck, which she had been allowed to wear while Miranda finished dressing. It had been set with real emeralds when her mother first owned it, but their finances had forced her to sell the gems and replace them with paste. The paste stones were rather unnaturally colored and fitted badly into their settings, but Miranda liked the way they matched her eyes.

She tried to tell herself yet again that she ought not to try to impress anyone. Gerard's opinion of her appearance shouldn't interest her in the least, because she would never consider exposing her heart to someone else. No one had ever understood her, and there was too much about her that could never come to light.

She would always be who she was, she would always be *how* she was. So it would always be just herself.

"Shall we collect the other children and go downstairs?" she asked Ellie. The little girl jumped off the low cot on which Miranda had been temporarily sleeping while the house was so full of guests and servants.

The other nursery maids were herding children out of the other bedrooms in the nursery wing, and Miranda helped wipe hands and faces with a damp cloth, retie sashes that had gone askew, and find a couple of lost shoes. Then they all went down to the drawing room.

Even though she was surrounded by excited children and all the family gathered for dinner, she looked up and met Gerard's eyes as soon as she entered the room. His injury had caused him to lose some weight, but he still stood tall and proud, exuding a vitality that made all other men look weak and sickly. His dark evening coat set off his wide shoulders, and his snowy cravat was simply tied with modest shirt points, which revealed the strong line of his jaw.

He smiled at her, which made her blush and look away. Then she was embarrassed to have responded in so missish a fashion.

There was a cry as two boys began to argue over who would get the largest piece of roast beef at dinner, and she turned her attention to her charges.

She dissuaded some of the children from starting a game of jack straws, since they were to dine soon, and directly on time, the butler opened the drawing room doors to announce that dinner was served. While the other guests proceeded into the dining room, Miranda kept a watchful eye on Paul, who delighted in playing with the greenery over the fireplace and had already caused an entire bough to tumble to the floor this morning after church.

She was one of the last to be seated, and she saw an opportunity. Her grand-aunt Lavinia had arrived only this morning, and the elderly woman had traded seats with someone—most likely offending Felicity's sense of propriety—and was near to the children's chairs. Miranda traded seats with Paul in order to sit next to her grand-aunt.

"Hello, Aunt Lavinia."

"Oh! Catherine—no, Miranda, isn't it? You look just like your mother," Aunt Lavinia shouted. She was not the oldest person at table, but she probably had the worst sense of hearing. However, she could read lips, so Miranda made an effort to face her when speaking.

"Have you been enjoying yourself, Aunt?"

"Most certainly, dear. So many friends have returned to the neighborhood for Christmas, so in the next few days, I shall call upon them."

And, knowing her aunt, gossiping and collecting news. She was sister to Miranda's grandfather and had married Sir Justin Skinnerton, whose estate bordered the Belmoore lands. A lifelong resident of the area, she was close to all the local families.

Cecil *harrumphed* enough that silence slowly filtered down the long table until all eyes were upon him. Then he gave a most respectful prayer, giving thanks for the food, for the Christ child, for the past harvest, for the harvest to come, for everyone's good health, for everyone's continued good health, and he might have continued if Paul had not whispered loudly, "When can we eat?"

Cecil cleared his throat and concluded his prayer, then stood. It signaled the servants to scurry about and serve steaming cups of wassail to all the company, including a special version using apple cider instead of ale for the children. Extra servants had been hired for the ball after dinner, so it only took a minute or two before everyone had a cup to raise.

"A toast to family and friends," Cecil said solemnly.

The company replied, "Family and friends!" and drank.

Miranda savored the flavor of the sweet wassail, a secret recipe passed down to each of the baronets' wives in the Belmoore family. Felicity had made the wassail every year since Cecil's mother had died, and Miranda admitted Felicity had a knack for it. She perhaps used less ale and more sherry, which brought out the flavors of the roasted apples, nutmeg, and ginger.

The servants began to serve the food, and Miranda was hard-pressed to keep Paul, seated on her other side, from taking an entire leg of pheasant onto his plate. There was also roast beef, venison, goose, pork, pigeons, chicken, and fish. Miranda forced Paul to take some vegetables, which was much less difficult than it might have been had there not been so many to choose from, including carrots, lettuces, parsnips, celery, leeks, and cabbage.

Paul attacked his plate like a savage. Miranda considered admonishing him, but then decided that surely bad table manners were excused at Christmastide. Instead, she turned to her grand-aunt. "Did Mrs. Seager's son and his family come up from London to have Christmas with her?" She did not wish to open with the question she most wanted answered, and hoped to distract her aunt with her favorite topic—her neighbors' affairs.

"No, not this year, for they were promised to his wife's family. Mrs. Seager was feeling quite low when I spoke with her last week. And her nephew is in the navy, apparently fighting off a horde of mosquitoes in India, so her family gathering is small this year."

Aunt Lavinia rambled on, not only about Mrs. Seager's family, but also about the Drews, the Barnes, and the Wilsons as her mind wandered down its twisting trail of news.

During a lull in the conversation, Miranda asked, "Aunt, would any of your friends perhaps have need of a companion or governess?" She would prefer to accompany Ellie to the Foremont home, but she must still continue to search for a paid position that would enable her to escape Felicity, or the Beattys.

Her aunt's eyebrows rose as her fork halted halfway to her mouth. "Good to see some pluck in you after all, my dear."

Miranda smiled. "You will not mention this to Cecil?"

"Good gracious, why should I do that? I try to avoid speaking to the blockhead as often as possible. And his termagant of a wife is just as bad."

"I do wish to find a position as soon as may be, perhaps even before Twelfth Night."

"I know of nothing at the moment, my dear, but I shall speak to my friends about it when I visit them. You should have written to me earlier."

"I feared Cecil would intercept your reply."

"Ah, yes, the nosy man still goes through all the post, does he? He's just like his father."

Except that Cecil's mother had been a soft woman,

indolent but not unkind. Felicity had run roughshod over her mother-in-law.

"Have you spoken to the rector's new wife?" Aunt Lavinia asked. "Mrs. Barnes wrote to tell me all about her. Mrs. Peterson apparently married to disoblige her well-connected family, at least until her husband's older brother unexpectedly became heir presumptive to an earldom. She may have friends in need of a companion or governess."

"I believe she is attending the ball tonight." Miranda need only attend to the children after dinner before she could return downstairs to the ball.

Miranda had not attended the ball last Christmas, during her first year with Cecil after her parents died. Felicity's youngest son had developed a putrid sore throat and so Miranda had nursed him throughout Christmas Day. He had complained bitterly at missing the Christmas pudding.

"Speaking of Mrs. Barnes, her great-nephew is now a lieutenant in the army," Aunt Lavinia said. "She just heard from him in a letter. He was foolish enough to be bitten by a dog. She is quite concerned, for she wrote to me, 'Lavinia, you never know about these foreign dogs. They may carry exotic diseases.' And I must say, I do believe she is correct."

Finally, the servants removed the dinner dishes and the candles were extinguished. The children began squirming in their seats and whispering to each other.

With dramatic flair, the butler entered the dining room bearing the large, mounded Christmas pudding on a platter, aflame with a blazing blue light, with flickers of scarlet and orange. Miranda could smell the burning brandy, which also carried the scent of citrus peel and sugar. The adults applauded while the children cheered. Carefully, the butler set the pudding on the table.

The enormity of the pudding ensured that everyone had a generous portion. As happened every year, there were cries of delight and dismay as people found on their plates the trinkets that had been stirred into the pudding. This year, Felicity was delighted to find the silver shilling, signifying wealth, while Lady Wynwood found the button for a lucky life, and one of Aunt Augusta's younger sons was disgusted by the ring he found, which predicted marriage. Perhaps most appropriately, Gerard received the miniature anchor, meaning safe harbor found.

Paul eyed Miranda's plate, which had a larger portion of pudding than his own, so she traded with him. And then her fork hit something hard, and she pulled out the silver thimble.

She stared at it. Although she knew it was only a game, just a silly tradition, she wanted to burst into tears—she, who tried never to show her emotions, to simply present a mask of calm to all the world, as if the barbs and stings did not bother her in the least. This barb was perhaps one of the worst, and yet it was entirely accidental.

One of the children crowed, "Miranda's got the thimble!"

There was a single heartbeat of surprised, uncomfortable silence around the table. Then Miss Church-Pratton giggled.

Felicity quickly hissed at her, and she was silenced, but her laughter caused some of the children to mimic her. Sniggers and whispers erupted, and while one or two adults hushed their children, they responded slowly to the reprimands.

Miranda's face flamed like the brandy-soaked pudding. Yet why should she be embarrassed? She was a spinster, as the thimble signified, and it was no secret that such was her fate. Her own parents had not been able to induce a man to offer for her when she had had a dowry, before the crops had failed and her father mortgaged the farm.

But a clawed hand gripped her heart, squeezing and digging into it. She closed her eyes, focused on her breathing, tried once more to reclaim the equanimity that was the only comfort she now had.

She opened her eyes. She picked up the thimble with fingers that shook only a little and wiped it with her napkin. She said the first thing that came to mind. "How fortuitous. I had need of a new thimble."

A different type of laughter rippled along the table, with perhaps some relief that the moment had passed.

She did not know why, but she dared to look down the table at Gerard. He was staring at her, his eyes thunderous, concerned.

Miranda held his gaze, then gave a small smile. The lines along his brow relaxed, although he did not smile back.

"Good show, my girl." Aunt Lavinia patted her hand. "The thimble is not only for spinsterhood. It also is for thrift, a woman who saves."

She gave a short bark of laughter, which might have had a hint of hysteria in it. "I have no money to save, Aunt Lavinia. And no household to save it for."

"It is not always money. Women save many things."

A small hand crept into hers from her other side. She turned to meet Paul's fierce look.

"When I am old enough, I shall marry you, Cousin Miranda," he said. "Then they shall see they ought not to have laughed."

"You darling boy." She kissed the top of his head and wrapped her arm around him briefly.

Then she bent low to whisper in his ear. "Let's play Snapdragon near Miss Church-Pratton's skirt."

Chapter Eight

Gerard had been helpless. Too helpless to do anything for her.

He had wanted to shout at them all to stop laughing at her, or perhaps go to her, take her hand, and pull her from the dining room. But anything of the sort would only embarrass her further.

He saw the pain in her eyes, and he saw the mask of calm settle over her face. He had never fully realized it was a mask until that moment.

There was a great deal about her that he didn't know. That he hadn't cared to know.

He wanted to know all those things now.

Perhaps not at this exact moment. First he had to walk again, properly, without this cursed cane. He wanted to be whole again, and independent, and regain some measure of self-respect.

Also at this exact moment, he had to somehow escape the two chattering women on either side of him before his ears bled.

He sat at the edge of the ballroom as couples swirled to the strains of a country dance. Garlands of greenery draped the walls in graceful arcs, lending the scent of the woodlands to the room, while servants moved about with cups of wassail or punch or wine. Everyone in the county who had been invited had come for the Belmoores' annual Christmas ball.

However, the two women sitting next to him affected to have no interest in dancing. Miss Church-Pratton was charming, but he noticed that the conversation invariably circled round to herself or something related to herself. Miss Barnes was not so self-centered—she asked him question upon question about his life and interests and thought everything he did was wonderful.

Gerard felt trapped in more ways than one. He used to love dancing. He hadn't been terribly good at it, but he had enjoyed it. He enjoyed watching it much, much less.

His knee ached as if to remind him, *You're landlocked, my boy.*

"Such a crush," Miss Church-Pratton said. "I am sure Felicity is thrilled at the attendance, but I prefer a smaller, more select party, myself."

"Did you attend any balls, Captain Foremont?" Miss Barnes asked. "I am sure you must have been quite popular."

He thought of his men, shirtless, dancing a jig on the upper deck. "Quite a few balls, I daresay."

He looked up suddenly and saw Miranda across the room. She was not looking at him, but appeared to be searching the ballroom for someone. When she saw him, she smiled slightly, then her gaze slid to the two ladies with him.

And he knew in that instant that he would not be

feeling this way if Miranda were sitting next to him instead.

Then someone walked into his line of sight and he could see her no longer.

"I much prefer sitting here with you, Captain Foremont," Miss Church-Pratton said. "The young country folk whom Felicity was forced to invite are so exuberant when they dance. The men quite crush one's dress."

"I am sure you would never do so, Captain," Miss Barnes said.

He thought of excusing himself on the grounds that he saw his mother signaling to him, but for the small problem that his mother was not in the ballroom and the fear that the two women would insist upon accompanying him to her.

Rescue came in the unlikely person of Lady Wynwood.

"Miss Barnes," Lady Wynwood said, "your mother may need your assistance in the drawing room. She is partnered with Mrs. Seager at Whist and is so frustrated that she looks as though she might wring her neck."

"Oh, goodness." Miss Barnes hurried off to prevent her parent from committing murder.

Lady Wynwood settled into her vacated seat. "Miss Church-Pratton, Captain Foremont, lovely ball, is it not? It puts me in mind of one I attended during my come-out in London. I was thrilled to be asked to dance by the most handsome boy in the room—Lord Kellerton, before he lost all his lovely golden hair and contracted the pox from his mistress."

Gerard choked, and Miss Church-Pratton looked scandalized. Lady Wynwood was up to some sort of trick.

"I had enhanced my *décolletage* with some, er, strategically tucked muslin. We were engaged in a lively country dance, when a piece of muslin became *untucked.* You can imagine my consternation, Miss Church-Pratton. How to explain the unevenness of one's bosom?"

Lady Wynwood stopped and looked expectantly at Miss Church-Pratton, obviously waiting for a response. The young lady actually gulped and said weakly, "Indeed."

Gerard was forced to look away, his face flaming, unsure if he would perish from embarrassment or break a rib from holding in his laughter. He saw Miranda again. She was still looking for someone, her gloved hand fingering the paste stones at her throat that made her eyes glow like real emeralds. Compared to the more richly dressed women, she looked fresh and unspoiled, and more lovely.

But then Felicity appeared, her mouth pinched. She gripped Miranda by the elbow and dragged her out of the ballroom.

Gerard tensed, and realized he had been about to rise to go after her, rudely leaving Lady Wynwood and Miss Church-Pratton. Something about Miranda made him want to throw off all the conventions of polite society.

"Look at Mrs. Drew, glaring daggers at me," Lady Wynwood said. "She and my mother are mortal enemies, did you know?"

"If your mother is anything like yourself, I find it hard to believe anyone could dislike her," Gerard said.

"Oh, you rogue." Lady Wynwood squeezed his arm.

"A year or two ago, at a rout, she and my mother had such a row that Mrs. Drew began waving her cane about, and she popped a poor young man between the legs."

Miss Church-Pratton made a strangled sound. Her face had turned a dark puce color that clashed with her pink dress. She plied her fan frenetically and her gaze darted about the ballroom with desperation.

The country dance ended, and a young man approached, one of the squire's sons. He was a stout lad, full of his own consequence and certain he was the catch of the county. "Miss Church-Pratton, are you free for the next dance?"

"*Yes*." She nearly dragged him out to form one of the sets.

"Good gracious," Lady Wynwood said. "I thought I would need to start reciting the contents of my linen closet before she would leave."

Gerard turned his guffaw into a cough. "She probably would have remained if you had spoken of something so tame as your linen closet."

"Young people these days are so starched up. We were much more scandalous in my time, I assure you. That was quite entertaining. I am so glad Miranda sent me to you."

Miranda had known exactly how to rescue him. Gerard was grateful to her, and yet also a bit ashamed because he had not been able to help her in her acute time of need.

"I have spoken to your mother, Gerard," Lady Wynwood said. "I believe she may be more concerned about Miranda's status as a single young woman living under your roof."

The ballroom grew suddenly stifling. "I offered to move to Foremont Lacy."

"It is too near." Lady Wynwood regarded him shrewdly. He feared for a moment that she would bring up his marital plans, but she apparently changed her mind. "I shall speak to her again. We must not give up hope. Now, help me to the sofa in the drawing room. Miss Barnes's chair is terribly uncomfortable."

"You could have ordered Miss Church-Pratton to relinquish her seat rather than Miss Barnes," he said with a smile.

"I chose Miss Barnes because it was easier to send her away," Lady Wynwood said as Gerard took her arm and helped her to her feet. "Miss Church-Pratton is remarkably stubborn. Just like her mother. One day I shall tell you all about it."

He gave her his arm, and she entertained him with disreputable stories about herself and others, which he was not entirely certain were truthful, until they walked between the open double doors to the drawing room and he deposited her upon a sofa. "May I fetch anything for you, my lady?"

"No. I shall send one of my young cousins to procure me a cup of wassail and add a splash more sherry to it. One of them is sure to know where Cecil keeps his secret cache."

Gerard obliged her by signaling to one of Mrs. Hathaway's sons to attend to her before he returned to the ballroom. As he did, he noticed Felicity returning to the room, her face the mask of the gracious hostess, but without Miranda. He waited, but she did not appear behind Felicity.

The dance was nearing its end, and he did not wish to be trapped again by Miss Church-Pratton, so he quickly exited the room to search for Miranda. He had not looked forward to the ball, although he was obliged to attend, and he had not predicted the company of Miss Church-Pratton, whom he had assumed would dance with all the young men. He would rather speak to Miranda. And then perhaps he would retire rather than watching the rest of the dancing.

He looked down the hallway outside the ballroom, but at first he saw no one. Then he peered into the shadows at the end of the hallway, and saw a figure leaning against the wall. He headed toward her.

It was only when he drew near that he realized something was wrong. Her hand over her stomach trembled. Her face was whiter than the painted walls.

"Miranda."

She saw him, and something in her eyes made him think of the faces of men who were drowning.

He strode forward, his cane dropping to the ground, and he folded her in his arms.

Chapter Nine

At first, Miranda was too startled and too distraught to think. She could only feel. The fine wool of his coat against her cheek, his hand at her waist, the other at her back, pressing her close. The smell of mint, and somehow, the wildness of the sea.

A sudden burst of women's laughter from the open door to the ballroom down the hallway made them both jump apart. And yet even out of his embrace, Miranda still felt ... anchored.

She couldn't look at him. He would see her pain, scraped raw by too many months in this house, and her desperation as she tried to snatch at the unraveling threads of who she was.

"What is it, Miranda?"

She simply shook her head.

The music from the ballroom drifted to them, lilting strains in counterpoint to laughter and gaiety. She felt more detached from life than she ever had before, standing here in the hallway while her family and neighbors danced and enjoyed themselves. Even if she were not unhappy, that sort of society was not hers. She was too different to ever belong.

Gerard picked up his cane, seized her hand, and pulled her down the hallway, away from the ballroom.

"What are you doing?" she hissed.

"Neither of us wishes to be anywhere near *that*." He tilted his head back towards the open doorway, and she heard the bitter edge in his voice. When she had seen him in the ballroom earlier, he had clearly been annoyed by his two female companions, but his gaze had also strayed to the dancers. Even at fourteen years old, he had loved romping around the dance floor with the Belmoore cousins. She knew that sitting with Miss Church-Pratton and Miss Barnes had been difficult for him in more ways than one.

So she let him drag her down the hallway to the servants' stairs at the back. They exited from the side door and skirted the house to the formal gardens.

The night sky was dark with the new moon, but Felicity had arranged for lanterns and torches to light the gardens, perhaps to dissuade guests from scandalous behavior by attempting to illuminate any dark corners. She needn't have worried because the air was too sharp for any to venture from the overheated ballroom.

Gerard led her next to a bright torch burning in a stand at the edge of the garden, so that the warmth from the fire kept them from shivering in the cold air. Above them and to their left came the sounds from the ballroom, but directly above them and to their right, all was darkness and quiet on the long, deserted balcony.

"It is too cold, Gerard." Then she wished she hadn't spoken because he removed his tailcoat, which sat loosely upon his shoulders, and draped it around her. It held his warmth and his scent, and she felt he was embracing her again.

"You mustn't." She was both scandalized and intrigued to see him in his waistcoat and shirtsleeves.

"After years at sea, the cold does not affect me as it once did." Indeed, he wasn't even shivering. "Do you remember that Christmas I found you alone in the woods? I gave you my coat then, also."

"And then, as now, I had wanted to be alone," she said with a hint of steel.

"You *said* you wished to be alone, but then you confessed that Cecil had called you a lackwit, and so I darkened his daylights for him."

"Of course you would remember that." Eight-year-old Gerard had been grinning and Cecil had been crying as they tussled on the front lawn.

"Whose daylights shall I darken for you now? Felicity's?"

"Oh, Gerard, do not speak nonsense."

"What did she say to you?"

"It is silly." She swallowed. "She was embarrassed by my dress. And my necklace. She expressed herself better than I expected—she said that she had not realized I had no appropriate attire this year for the ball or she would have given me one of her old gowns, but it was too late now. She didn't wish me to return to the ballroom because one or two of the local women had been whispering about me."

"How dared she?" The cold would certainly not bother him now—he was on fire with indignation. "You are her responsibility."

"I was hurt because I quite like my gown," Miranda

said. "It is my favorite."

There was a pause, then he suddenly gave a reluctant low laugh. "Miranda, you always know what to say to diffuse my temper."

"Not always. You still engaged in fisticuffs with Cecil."

"I don't like the way they treat you."

A part of her was comforted by his words, but another part of her was frustrated by him, because she didn't understand why he was acting like this. "Why would you care how they treat me?"

He was surprised by her question. "Because it is all so unjust."

"There is a great deal of injustice in this world, Gerard."

"I cannot stand by and do nothing." He flinched, as if remembering something, then added, "At dinner, I should have ... If I had been ..."

"Gerard, you feel guilt for things which have nothing to do with you." It was making it more difficult for her to distance her feelings from him. She removed his coat to hand it to him, and the cold sliced through her gown. "You must return."

He shrugged it back on with her help, but then he took her hand. Even through their gloves, she felt his warmth.

"I feel as though I am still at sea and need a war to fight," he said.

"You are already helping me. I shall leave Wintrell Hall with you and your parents, and then I shall go to Cousin Laura's home." She did not tell him that she would try to find a position. She did not wish to be dependent even upon Cousin Laura. "I am not your war,

Gerard."

"I know that, but ..." His fingertips touched her face. In the light from the torch, he looked confused.

She didn't want him to be confused, because it only made *her* feel more confused. She closed her eyes and turned her cheek away. "Gerard—"

He took her chin, angling it back toward him, and then he was kissing her.

It was everything she had always dreamed it would be, and even better. His mouth was firm, and his hand snaked around her waist to the small of her back, pulling her closer to him. He kissed her as though she were precious to him, as though she meant something to him.

It was the first time she had been kissed. In all her girlhood, she had not been inclined to allow any boy such liberties while she yet pined for the young man away at sea, and as she grew older, the number of boys who wanted to kiss her had dwindled.

But those had been girlish fantasies, and she was now older and wiser. And no matter how she might wish it, this was no longer that idealized young man.

She pulled away just as he did. "Gerard."

"I beg your pardon, Miranda." He looked shocked at his own behavior. "I ought not to have ... I respect you a great deal ..."

She drew upon all her strength, her deepest calm. "It was a mistake, easily forgotten." She shivered. "We must go inside. I am cold."

"Of course." He offered her his arm and led the way back to the servants' door.

The silence was awkward, and he broke it to say, "In the ballroom, you looked as though you were searching for someone."

"Mrs. Peterson."

"The rector's wife?"

"I wish to ask her if she knows of any families in need of a companion or governess. In the event that you and Cousin Laura cannot convince your mother to allow me to accompany Ellie."

He opened his mouth, but then closed it without speaking. Then he said, "You cannot speak to Mrs. Peterson tonight. She left an hour ago. The rector was feeling ill."

"Oh." And Miranda had spent that time looking for her, bringing herself to Felicity's notice. She would find a moment to go to the rectory tomorrow.

She felt Gerard's arm stiffen under her fingers, and that was all the warning she was given before they were attacked.

Two men peeled themselves from the shadows, one on either side of them. Miranda gasped, then berated herself for not screaming to alert the servants as the man closest to her lunged for her. The other man swung a meaty fist at Gerard.

But Gerard ducked to avoid the blow and his cane came up to slash at the man. The attacker just barely avoided the tip of the cane connecting with his temple.

Miranda's attacker had grabbed her hard around the waist. Her corset was not tightly laced, but it prevented her from twisting out of his grasp and it made it hard for her to draw breath for a scream. She tried to shout but it sounded feeble, and the man clamped a calloused, dirt-smeared hand over her mouth. She smelled grime and rotting meat, and gagged.

She kicked at him, but her slippers caused scant damage to his boot-encased legs. Flailing her arms only made him grunt and squeeze her waist more tightly. She couldn't breathe, and her vision began to darken at the edges.

She then thought to bite at the finger nearest her mouth. She tasted blood and dirt.

The man cried out and pulled his hand away. She drew the largest breath she could and screamed. Her attacker stiffened.

Gerard did not stop battling the other man. He wielded his cane like a sword, jabbing and swinging it in almost invisible arcs. But then a misstep on the flagstones caused his knee to wobble, and he stumbled.

His attacker saw his weakened knee and kicked at it.

Gerard cried out, the sound ringing off the outside walls of the house and the tall windows on the first floor. His face tight with pain, he fell to the ground. The man kicked at his knee again but missed, his boot sliding off Gerard's shin.

Miranda had been kicking backward with her feet, at first hampered by her gown. Then her heel swung up and connected with something soft.

The man dropped her abruptly, and she tumbled to the ground. He clutched between his legs, his round face contorted with rage. He aimed a kick at her, but it was feeble and she rolled to avoid it.

Suddenly the servants' door opened and two footmen ran out into the garden. They caught sight of the two men and shouted.

The attackers fled, using the shadows of the trees and bushes to disappear into the night. One of the footmen ran after them, but the other went to Miranda.

"I'm well. See to Captain Foremont," she said.

Her heart clogged her throat. Gerard lay on the ground, clutching his knee, his face deathly white.

Chapter Ten

December 26th

The day after the attack, Gerard awoke early in the morning to stabbing pain in his entire leg. His knee had swelled as large as the Christmas pudding, and the throbbing had kept him from falling asleep.

He had never been a docile patient, but injury had always made him feel like a baited bear, and inclined to roar just as loudly. Such was his peevish temper when his father's valet, Maddox, entered his bedroom earlier than usual. Gerard should have been grateful he had come, but the agony in his knee had somehow traveled up his body into a headache raging against the backs of his eyeballs.

"What do you want?" he demanded.

"I have a poultice, sir, sent by Miss Miranda."

"Well, you can take it away," he said perversely. He ought to do something to alleviate the pain in his knee, yet at the same time he wanted to be left alone to suffer in silence.

"I believe she rose early this morning to make this for

you, sir," Maddox said, unimpressed by his master's son's ill temper.

"Oh, very well."

The valet folded back the sheets and gently rolled up his nightclothes to expose his knee. The cool air seemed to make the injured limb hiss. Then Maddox retrieved the cloth-wrapped bundle he'd brought into the room and laid it on Gerard's bare skin.

"Maddox, that's an icicle!" he roared. "I thought poultices were warm."

"It's what Miss Miranda gave to me, sir."

It was uncomfortable, and it did nothing to improve his mood, although his knee felt slightly better after Maddox removed the poultice.

"Shall I fetch breakfast for you, sir?"

"No. I refuse to remain swaddled in bedclothes all day."

The valet did not quite roll his eyes at him, but his expression clearly indicated his master's son deserved a proper scolding. "Very good, sir."

However, when he attempted to walk from his bed to the dressing table, he only barely made it to the chair in front of the fireplace before collapsing, his knee throbbing and sweat running in rivulets down his face. The realization that his cane was no longer sufficient to support him made him want to fling it across the room, except for the fact that he didn't want to have to crawl to reclaim it in order to get back into bed.

"Perhaps if you would return to bed, sir?"

"Leave me alone, Maddox," he barked.

However, at that moment came a gentle knock at the door behind him. He heard it open, and then Miranda's voice said, "These are for your master, Maddox. I found them in the nursery attics." The door had closed by the time Gerard twisted around to see what she'd brought.

Maddox held a pair of crutches. A more cowardly retainer would have acted with more caution, but Maddox bore the crutches aloft like a gift presented to the king.

Gerard was about to tell him where he could fling them, but bit his tongue. He exhaled long and low, then said, "Bring them here." How had Miranda guessed the cane would no longer suffice?

The crutches were a trifle short, but they had been carved with wide stumps, no doubt to allow them to be used with ease out of doors. He ought to be grateful for Miranda's thoughtfulness, but they were a bitter reminder that he had cast crutches aside for his cane weeks ago, but must now take them up again.

Dressing was more of an ordeal than he anticipated, and he resentfully stumped out of his bedroom, determined not to remain cooped up despite his injury.

Miranda was in the hallway with Ellie. Waiting for him.

"'Randa said you would not stay in bed," Ellie said to him. "Let's play jack straws."

"I did not come out of my room to play jack straws," he replied grumpily.

"You came out of your room to test your new crutches," Miranda said, calm and cheerful. "Let us walk with Gerard, Ellie."

And of course he lasted no farther than the drawing room, where the women had gathered with embroidery and knitting while the men were out shooting. They erupted in cries of dismay and fluttered about as he sank onto a settee, cosseting him as if he were a babe.

"You shouldn't be up and about," Mrs. Hathaway scolded him.

"To think those men would attack you in the garden, of all places," another woman said.

"They might have invaded the house and murdered us all in our beds."

"They were more likely after the silver. Probably aided by an unscrupulous servant."

"Well, Cecil has at least instructed the servants to be more vigilant in guarding the house."

"Captain Foremont, here is a cushion for your foot," Miss Church-Pratton said.

"It's his knee that's bothering him, not his foot, you ninny," said Lady Skinnerton acidly.

Miranda, the wretch, stood to one side and watched him, smiling faintly at his chagrin. It was as though she could read his mind—he'd rather have played jack straws with Ellie. She had known he wouldn't have the strength in his knee to make it to any other room in the house. Then she and Ellie left him to the tender ministrations of Miss Church-Pratton and Mrs. Hathaway.

*

Gerard flattered himself that he was not a complete donkey-head and agreed to take a dinner tray in his room. He thought the solitude would appeal to him, but the knock on the door as he finished eating roused his spirits.

"Come," he called.

The door opened and Miranda peeked inside. "I have

brought Maddox, and another poultice, and Ellie."

"You will remain outside whilst I apply it, Miss Miranda," Maddox said as he stepped into the room.

"I have seen your master in his shirt-sleeves often enough when we were children."

"You are children no longer, Miss Miranda." And Maddox closed the bedroom door.

His words reminded Gerard of last night—not the attack, but what had happened just before. He knew he ought to regret it, but he did not. Kissing Miranda had made him feel more anchored than any other time since he'd been back in England, even when he was home with his parents.

His emotions had been in turmoil because he was not whole, and while he was not as mad with frustration as he had been when he'd first awakened in the hospital, he yet resented the situation with all his being. He could not subject any woman to this, especially not Miranda, whom he had known nearly all his life.

And yet he had kissed her, a woman who was not his, who could not be his.

Maddox applied the poultice, which was blessedly warm this time, then covered his master's limbs properly before allowing Miranda and Ellie to enter the bedroom. He left them with the door wide open.

"Isn't it past your bedtime, miss?" Gerard said to Ellie.

"I wanted to play jack straws with you," she said, climbing onto his bed to sit beside him. She wore a dressing gown that was too large for her.

Miranda settled into a chair nearby. "Ellie could not sleep, so I brought her with me."

So he played jack straws with Ellie.

"You are cheating, miss," he said after the first game.

"Am not." Ellie yawned.

"I fear she learned to cheat from Paul," Miranda said.

He gave Ellie a mock frown. "You are also a competitive little Captain Sharp."

"*That* she learned from Cousin Laura."

In the middle of the second game, Ellie curled up on the bedclothes and went to sleep, her mouth slightly open, and breathing with a little whistle.

Gerard stared at her. "I must say that no woman has found me such a bore that she fell asleep on my bed." He did not realize how warm that sounded until it came out of his mouth. He had been too long at sea, or perhaps he was simply too awkward with his tongue.

But Miranda was not offended, nor was she flustered by the scandalous comment—she simply began to pick up the jack straws. "Perhaps you are being repaid for a woman's broken heart," she said lightly.

"I have not broken any hearts while at sea."

Miranda did not reply, but gave him a sidelong look. Perhaps it was the bright color of her eyes, but he had never before seen an expression of greater incredulity.

"Upon my honor, I have not." He had stolen a few kisses, certainly, all from women in foreign ports, but he had never compromised any of them—and several had been the ones to kiss him. He did not even know how to deliver those pretty speeches that women seemed to like.

But with Miranda, he had no need of pretty speeches. He could converse with her with ease. She did not make him feel uncomfortable or like a bumbling youth, as Miss Church-Pratton did.

And yet he had given her a gross insult, because she was a gently bred, respectable young woman. "Miranda," he said slowly, "about last night, before the attack."

"We agreed it was forgotten." She turned her face from him so that he only saw the curve of her cheek, but she was cool and composed. It was as if the kiss had never happened. But then he saw the rapid rise and fall of her chest, and knew she was not unaffected. She was simply uncommunicative about it.

"Miranda, I am obligated—"

"No, you are not." Her voice was higher than usual. "I beg you, put the events of last night from your mind. Or at least ... *those* events." She added, "Cecil is quite put out with us."

"As if we were somehow to blame?"

"Cecil does not wish to appear indifferent, but he also has no wish to ride about the countryside searching for the two attackers, when he knows he will not find them. He does not like the way the situation makes him appear to the neighbors."

"Save me from Cecil's pride," he groaned.

"Were the men who attacked us in league somehow with the woman in the woods?"

He had been wondering the same. "I don't know. The men could be her cronies, or she may have hired them."

"They attacked both of us. Was I still their target?" Her fingers tightened briefly on the jack straws.

"There is no way to know. Perhaps they were not connected to the woman and I was their target."

"You? But why?"

He shrugged. "I am simply a post-captain who lost his

last ship. I have no influence, no inheritance of any worth."

"But what of your property inherited from your grandmother? And also your father's property?"

"In the event of my death, it all goes to my cousin, who already owns an estate twice as large."

"Is there a possibility that the two men could be related to a man who died under your command?"

He thought of all the men who had died—too many faces. "Perhaps, but ... I have been in the Royal Navy for sixteen years. There have been dozens of men who lost their lives."

"But no one attempted to end yours while you were in the hospital in London," she said. "If I wished to kill you, I would do it then, whilst you were weak or unconscious. Or I would contrive to poison your food. No one would know."

He raised an eyebrow at her. "Miranda, I shall be sure never to incur your wrath. You are positively bloodthirsty."

She ignored him. "Also, you were not attacked at home with your parents. This only happened when you arrived here."

"So perhaps the two men live here. I must make inquiries to discover if anyone has lost a loved one at sea."

"You said you had a servant who could ask the local men whether anyone is newly come to the area."

"I have sent for someone, but he has not yet arrived. Now he will have two pieces of information to ferret out."

Miranda tucked the jack straws in a pocket of her

gown and moved around the bed to collect Ellie's sleeping figure. "Those men could have attacked you because you were with me."

"But they could have harmed you or taken you, and they did neither."

She frowned as she carefully gathered Ellie into her arms. "I do not like that so much is unknown." She froze. "Oh, dear."

"What is it?" Had she thought of something he had not?

She nodded toward the bedclothes.

Ellie had driveled in a large wet spot in the middle of his bed.

Chapter Eleven

December 27th

After Miranda had put the children to bed after dinner, she entered the drawing room and immediately saw Gerard in the far corner. It seemed she could always find him in a crowded room, which was why she had noticed that he had seemed preoccupied all day.

It was more than the seriousness of the situation or frustration that the men who had attacked them had not yet been found. There was a deadness in his eyes and an increased tension along his jaw, which made her concerned about him. It was as though he was in deep pain, but not from his body.

Tonight, he sat with his mother while a large number of the party played at charades in front of the roaring fire. His mother watched the players and laughed at their wild antics, but Gerard barely looked at them. He was not stiff, but he was stern. His mother occasionally spoke to him, but it was obvious to Miranda that they were both irritated, although perhaps for different reasons.

Miranda had never seen Gerard like this, but she imagined this would be his expression as he stood on board his ship, the implacable captain.

She sailed across the room. "Mrs. Foremont, I know how much you enjoy music. Wouldn't you like to join the glee that is forming?" Several of the older members of the party were gathering around the pianoforte for singing. "I should be happy to sit with Gerard."

"I do not need a nursery maid," he snapped.

"I fear I know not how else to behave since I *am* a nursery maid," Miranda said sweetly.

He glared at her, but with a touch less irritation than before.

His mother's mouth had fallen open as she looked first at Miranda, then at Gerard. Her surprise only lasted a moment, however, before she said, "There is no need, Miranda. My son is my responsibility."

Her cold words made him look away.

Mrs. Foremont had never before been unfriendly to Miranda, but perhaps it was her resistance to allowing Miranda to accompany Ellie that made her seem more aloof. Yet whatever the cause, and whatever the outcome, Miranda could not bear to allow Gerard to wallow in his foul temper. Just as she had felt compelled to interfere with him yesterday, she wished to see him smile today.

"Mrs. Foremont, do leave your curmudgeonly son to me," Miranda urged. "Although he needs a good clout to the head to knock him out of his ill mood, I shall do my best with rousing conversation."

"I should like to see you try," he growled.

"The clout or the rousing conversation?"

He glowered at her.

Mrs. Foremont's eyebrows rose as she regarded the two of them.

"Gerard, it is of no purpose for us to be at loggerheads, because I always win." Miranda gave him a superior smile.

Gerard grunted and put his chin on his fist.

Strangely, his mother looked stricken, as if by a thought that surprised her. But there was also a touch of meekness as she nodded to Miranda. "I leave you to your fate, Miranda." Then she added with a saucy gleam in her eye, "If only to keep from laughing in front of my son and putting him even more out of sorts."

Yes, there was the Mrs. Foremont Miranda was used to. Gerard's mother swept away and Miranda took her seat. "There, did that make you feel better?" she asked Gerard cheerfully.

"I am not a child."

"No, you are not. But you were upsetting your mother."

"It was not my behavior that was upsetting my mother," he said in a low voice.

"What do you mean?"

He shook his head, but she reached out to touch the back of his hand briefly, where it lay on the arm of the chair. "You look as though you have been abandoned," she said.

"I am hardly abandoned. On the contrary, I am never left alone."

"Not physically abandoned, but perhaps emotionally."

He moved his hand from hers. "You are mistaken."

But she knew she was not. She recognized that

expression because she had felt it herself for so many years. "While my parents were alive, I knew I was very different from them, and they could not understand me. So they stopped trying. And I felt abandoned."

A muscle in his neck spasmed once, then stilled.

"I know they loved me," she said, "and yet they were apart from me."

He was silent, and she said nothing. She had never confessed that to anyone, and yet she had just spoken as if spilling a glass of wine into his lap.

When he spoke, she could barely hear him over the glee singers at the pianoforte and the rowdy yelling of the charades players.

"They think I may have done something unsavory."

She had hardly expected that. "Of course you did nothing of the sort."

He looked at her, but she could not read his expression. "You believe me."

"I always believe you." She said it without thinking.

Then he smiled. She took a short breath, and then calmed herself.

"My mother asked what I had done to cause those men to attack me."

"Oh, Gerard."

"Lately, my mother and I are constantly at daggers drawn. But I had not expected her to know me so little that she would ask that."

"You have been away from your family for many years. And then you were in their company for your convalescence. You are no longer their little boy. You have changed—you can hardly help having changed—and perhaps it frightens them because you are now a man, and they are uncertain of who you are."

"*You* did not change."

"You are wrong. I am very different." She was no longer that schoolgirl, and yet she felt her woman's heart reaching out to him again as she had done when she was twelve.

Their eyes met, and held. He seemed frozen, but not surprised. He reached out, and while he did not quite cup her cheek, his fingertips trailed from her cheekbone down to her jaw. He touched her as if she were a delicate flower, the centerpiece of an arrangement. Except that she was nothing of the sort. She was Miranda, who had just blurted to him that she felt abandoned.

She turned her head away, and his hand dropped.

She knew all the reasons he would not choose her. She was impoverished and his family would not wish him to marry a fortune-hunter. He would not consider the complication of a relationship with any woman while his leg had not yet healed.

She knew all the reasons she should not feel this way. Too many people in her life had failed her, and she was not willing to take the risk with someone like Gerard, who could have any woman he wanted as his wife. She could never believe he could ever love her. She had always thought that perhaps something was broken inside of her, which prevented people from caring about her.

Which prevented her from being able to open herself to anyone.

And yet she could not stop herself from wanting him as she had always wanted him. He had always been brave and kind, and he was all that still, but the experiences of his life had given him a depth and understanding that had not been there before.

And she was falling in love with him all over again. She could not stop herself.

"Miranda?"

She had been drowning in her thoughts for too long. She forced a smile. "When will you return to Foremont Lacy?"

"It has been let because I was away at sea when I inherited it from my grandmother."

"You used to talk about what you would do when you inherited it, the improvements to the house and farm."

"Those were the boastings of a foolish boy." He gave a half-smile. "I know now that I know nothing of estate management."

"You can learn from your father. Isn't it like ordering your men aboard ship?"

"I suppose, but I would need to know the orders to give, else I would make the men completely bewildered." His gaze drifted to his knee. "I had thought I would do all this when I was older."

"Perhaps it is better to learn while you are young, and your father is young." She hesitated, then said, "I know you are unhappy on shore, but I think you could come to enjoy it."

"I shall have to, or life will be intolerable." His voice was sad and only slightly tinged with bitterness.

"You have always risen to challenges. This will be as great a challenge as any you have faced on board your ship. Are you averse to running the farm at Foremont Lacy?"

"Not at all. I always expected to do so, and eventually

take over my father's estate, too." His gaze fell on his knee again. "Perhaps you are right. I will be able to ride a horse soon and can follow my father and his steward."

She hadn't realized how tense her shoulders had become until they relaxed. She'd had no illusions that she would cheer him up immediately, but she'd hoped that the thought of Foremont Lacy as a place for him to escape would comfort him, especially now when he was hurting from the suspicions of his parents. "Or perhaps you will bowl along in a dogcart like Squire Bigsby used to do."

"Good old Squire Bigsby. I would need a dog as mangy as his."

"There is a litter in the stables. If you ask him, I am certain Cecil will give you the runt."

"I would expect no less from Cecil."

A roar of laughter from the charades players filled the room. However, when the noise had died, Gerard turned to her with an uncomfortable set to his shoulders. "Miranda, I know you did not wish to speak of this, but we must."

She knew what he wanted to speak about, and the flash of remembrance of his arms around her, his lips pressed to hers, involuntarily sent a tremble of joy through her. She did not expect to be kissed again in her lifetime, and Gerard's kiss would be her brightest memory. "We must forget it happened."

"We cannot hide in the closet like we used to do and let the world pass by outside," he said. "My actions have bound me to you. I will do the honorable thing."

It was her escape from Cecil and from the Beattys, and yet she wanted to be honorable as well. It would be wrong to trap him into marriage, a man who did not love her, who would resent her. A marriage of convenience would be all her convenience and none of his. He had no need of a wife, no desire for one.

And even aside from that, she didn't want the honorable thing from him. She wanted passion and a friendship deeper than any other. And yet perversely, she could not take that step to open herself up to anyone. She had simply been alone for too long. "Gerard, do you love me?"

She thought she knew what she would see in his eyes, and had steeled herself for it. But she hadn't expected the warmth of his surprise. He was speechless, and so she rushed forward. "Of course you do not. I will not shackle you to a woman you do not love. It is not what I wish."

"Miranda—"

"And Gerard, if you married me, your family would call me a fortune-hunter. Your mother would be so distressed."

"Miranda—"

"So I have refused your proposal. You are free."

He gave her a dry look. "I did not actually propose."

"Oh. Well, I have saved you the trouble."

"If you would allow me to put in a word edgewise, I would say—"

Some of the charades players suddenly called his name, and Miss Church-Pratton crossed the room to tug playfully at his arm. "Come join us, Captain, do, for we believe the next clue has something to do with water."

Miss Church-Pratton, of course, did not acknowledge Miranda's presence, and Gerard rose from his chair in response to her entreaties and those of the other family members. However, he surprised Miranda by leaning close to tell her, "We have not finished discussing this, Miranda."

He collected his crutches and made his way to the charades players. Miranda rose to leave the room, but he glanced at her as she paused in the doorway. It was as though he had reached out to touch her across that distance. Her heart pulsed faster.

She took a deep breath and then exited the room, almost running up the stairs.

Why couldn't her girlhood infatuation have simply withered away? Why must he be so noble, and she so fearful?

Because yes, she was afraid of him. She was afraid of opening her heart to him. She was afraid that Gerard's fondness for her would dry up into a brittle embrace like that of her parents.

She would be grateful to him and the Foremonts if they would allow her to stay with them, but she could not stay for long. Once Ellie was comfortable, once Lady Wynwood was able to take her, she would go. She would find a position far away. She would never see him again, until he was old and married.

She stifled the sob that caught painfully in her throat, and hurried up to the nursery.

Chapter Twelve

December 28th

The next morning, as Gerard lounged in bed wearing a banyan, Maddox asked in long-suffering accents, "Will you attend the skating party today, sir?"

He hesitated before answering. He had no wish to be cooped up, but he also had no wish to sit on the sidelines with the women, or worse, to be shoved about on the ice in a sled like an old man. It was also a jostling carriage ride to the particular lake that had frozen over enough for skating.

There was a knock at the door, and Maddox had no sooner opened it than Miranda's voice asked, "Is he giving you a bear garden jaw, Maddox? Or is he pouting and refusing to stir?"

"Neither, you heartless wench," Gerard shouted to the open door.

"I have another poultice," came the disembodied voice.

"I'll not have you freezing off my leg."

"This one is warm."

Gerard glowered at the doorway, then nodded to Maddox. The valet was not able to suppress a shudder as he took a cloth bag from Miranda. He bore it well ahead of himself, and Gerard understood why as he neared the bed. The cloth held a lump of steaming mash that smelled like boiled turnips and a mix of pungent herbs.

"That smells worse than the ones before," Gerard said.

The voice came from the doorway. "You would do well to be civil, Captain Foremont, lest Maddox accidentally spill that upon your person, allowing you to enjoy the aroma for yet longer."

The corner of Maddox's lips twitched, but his face remained impassive. "If you would, sir?"

Gerard pulled up his pantaloon leg and removed his stocking. However, as Maddox laid the mash on his knee, Gerard caught Miranda peeking into the bedroom. "Miranda!"

But she was extraordinarily unmoved by the sight of his bare limb. "Move it more over the leg muscle, Maddox," she said. Somehow her undisturbed countenance soothed him. Perhaps it was simply the lack of *fussing* that he appreciated.

Suddenly there was movement at the doorway and Miranda's head disappeared. He heard his mother's voice, "Miranda, what are you—oh good gracious!" His mother halted in the open doorway, looking first at Gerard on his bed and Miranda just outside the room.

Gerard froze. Even with his valet here, this was highly irregular.

His mother saw the poultice, still steaming, then

exhaled audibly. She swept into the room and promptly sat on the chair on the other side of Gerard's bed. "Pray, continue, Maddox."

Maddox finished wrapping the disgusting mash around Gerard's knee. The strong scent burned his nose hairs, but he admitted the aches lessened considerably.

"Good Lord, that smells like a rat died on your leg," his mother said.

"Thank you, madam," he said.

"So, Gerard," his mother said, for all the world as if a young, unmarried woman were not standing outside his bedchamber, "will you join the skating party today?"

He had not intended to subject himself to the ordeal, but something in her expression made him wonder if he ought to do so. And he had a sudden idea as to how he might use the skating party to enact a plan that had been rattling about in his head for the past two days. "Had you intended to go?" he asked her.

"I shall not skate, but I will sit with you if you desire. You could also ride in a sled. Cecil will be bringing two of them, I believe."

"Mrs. Foremont, you should ride in the sled with Mr. Foremont," Miranda called from the doorway. Of course, being Miranda, she would not act as any other person and pretend that she could not hear every word.

His mother tried to ignore her. "I should be glad to sit with you, especially now that ..."

The heaviness settled on his chest. As an adult, he ought not to be a burden to his parents, to his mother in particular. Just as he had started gaining more independence, the attack had cast him back to the same situation of over a month ago.

"I'm certain Gerard will not lack for friends to sit with him. Miss Church-Pratton, perhaps?" Miranda peeked inside, and the look she gave him was completely unexceptionable, but he caught the devilish glint in those green eyes.

"Oh, this is ridiculous," his mother said. "I refuse to converse with a doorway. Miranda, do come inside. Maddox, are you quite finished?"

"Indeed, madam." His father's valet covered his leg discreetly with a towel as Miranda entered the bedroom. She was more hesitant than she had been last night with Ellie, but she sat quietly next to his mother. Maddox moved away and remained standing next to the open door.

"You should not curtail your amusement, Mrs. Foremont," Miranda said. "As we know, Gerard becomes insufferable when his every whim is being fulfilled. We should not contribute to the dissolution of his moral character."

He burst into laughter.

His mother blinked at him, then glanced uncertainly at Miranda.

"There you have it, Mother," he said. "My immortal soul may be at risk."

"Do not be irreverent, Gerard," his mother scolded.

"I shall sit with him, ma'am," Miranda said. "Surely you would rather spend time with your husband than your ill-tempered son. I am willing to sacrifice my head so no one else need do so."

His mother hesitated, but then she suddenly smiled. She was more relaxed with him than she had been in a long time. "Gerard, I beg you not to bite Miranda's head off."

"I will be on my best behavior, I promise."

Miranda rose. "Maddox, please wait a few minutes more before removing the poultice. Then you may convey your tyrannical master to the coach."

"I am not a tyrant," Gerard said.

"Gerard, don't be ridiculous. Of course you are."

He scowled at her.

She smiled, gave an elegant curtsey to him and his mother, and left the room.

His mother left soon afterward. As Maddox helped him to dress, Gerard was forced to concede that his knee felt a great deal better. After giving the valet a message to send, Gerard used the crutches to make his way to his parents' coach, which would convey them to the lake. He was relieved to find his parents as his only companions, although it was because the cursed crutches were like another passenger inside.

The coach jostled over the rough road, but the ride was not long and when they disembarked, the sun had emerged from the clouds to shine brightly upon the ice of the lake. Thick forest surrounded them on all sides, making the lake seem more isolated.

Servants had gone before them, bringing skates and the two sleds that could be pushed about on the ice. They had also created fires near which people might warm themselves, and were heating cider and chocolate.

He was surprised to find Miranda not yet at the lake, especially because many of the children had come in the first coaches and were now darting about on the ice. He did not see Ellie, either.

Gerard managed to maneuver carefully on the icy

ground to one of the stone benches that had been built on the upward slope on the north end. He scanned the forest beyond, but saw no movement. Well, it would hardly do to have the trap he'd set be obvious, would it?

He had just dropped to the bench, his leg trembling, when another coach arrived and Ellie shot out of it, heading directly for the skaters.

"Ellie!" Miranda had emerged, but then she saw Lady Wynwood take Ellie in hand, helping her tie on her skates, and she relaxed. More children tumbled from the coach behind her, and she helped them with their skates.

In a few minutes, she had climbed up the small rise to sit beside him. "Isn't it a lovely day? How does your knee feel?"

"Better." He paused, then added, "I have not yet thanked you for the poultices. And the crutches."

"Am I forgiven, then?"

"For what?"

"For not ignoring the extent of your injury."

His brow knit, then smoothed. "Is that what I have been doing?"

"It is not an unusual failing. I often refuse to acknowledge to myself how ill I actually am." She looked out at the skaters on the lake. "I am sure there are many people who would prefer that you be here, injured, than at the bottom of the ocean."

"Yes." His doctor in London had warned Gerard of the possibility that he would never walk without a cane. But even though he knew he should be grateful, he only felt ...

"I know you feel shackled," she said.

His throat tightened, and he couldn't speak.

"I understand the feeling of being trapped," she added. "But I have to believe that it will not last forever."

"Do you feel trapped in Cecil's house?"

She sighed. "Not trapped. I am grateful that he took me in, but ..."

"Yes. *But*." He understood that feeling.

"I feel sometimes as though I am aboard a ship," she said.

"Do you?"

"We are all together in the nursery wing. I do not have days off, so I must take advantage of any time I can spend by myself."

"Miranda, even servants have days off."

"I am a servant who is not a servant."

He reflected on that. On board, it had been difficult to find time to himself, but they had not been on duty all the time. "Things will be better when you come to stay with us," he said.

But as soon as he said it, he realized he could not say with certainty that he could convince his mother. He knew Lady Wynwood had also been attempting to sway her, but after the attack in the garden, his mother had intimated that since Miranda had been there for both attacks, she could not allow her to accompany Ellie. He understood her concern, but was no closer to uncovering the truth. Had the two attacks been connected?

"Would someone wish to harm you?" he asked her.

She blinked several times before adjusting to the sudden change in topic. "I ... I can't think of anyone who would wish to do so. And I have been here with Cecil's family for nearly two years, but no one has attempted to harm me before this. There have been no mysterious accidents, such as those in gothic novels."

He had to smile at her comparison. "No evil uncle attempting to force you into a distasteful marriage?"

She laughed, and the sound rang out in the stillness of the woods behind them, mingling with the laughter from the group on the pond. Ellie, skating with Paul, turned at the sound, saw her, and waved.

Miranda waved back, then pulled her cloak more tightly around her. "I am happy the weather turned cold enough for the skating party. Ellie was quite looking forward to today."

It was then that he noticed her neck was bare. "Where is your scarf?" He remembered the gray one she'd worn during the greenery hunting party, which she'd used to staunch the blood on Ellie's forehead.

"It was too stained."

"Have you no other? Here." He unwound the red and black scarf from his neck and draped it around hers.

"I cannot take your scarf."

"Maddox, like a mother hen, gave me two." He pulled back the edge of his cloak to show the other scarf wound underneath. He then proceeded to tie it under her chin.

She had become still, as if she had stopped breathing, although she did not look at him. He was close enough to her to smell lavender and a hint of lemon. He might have taken longer than necessary to fasten the scarf, but he was reluctant to draw away from her.

He felt both rested and vibrantly alive when he touched her, even with the bulky scarf between them. It reminded him of the night of the Christmas ball, and the kiss they'd shared.

He wanted to kiss her again.

Last night, when she'd asked him if he loved her, for one glorious moment, he had considered saying yes. It had been completely mad but completely wonderful.

But then reason had intruded. Of course he could not have come to love Miranda in only a few days. He had known her since they were children, and he was fond of her, that was the extent of it. His emotions—frustration, anger, bitterness, restlessness, sadness, and a hundred others he couldn't define—felt like the tangled silks in his mother's workbag. He had no room for romantic love.

"There," he said finally, and sat back.

"Thank you, Gerard."

He reminded himself of the reason he had attended the skating party, the reason he had positioned himself here at the most remote end of the lake.

As bait.

"Oh, goodness," she said. Paul had gotten into a squabble with Sally down on the lake. "I beg your pardon, Gerard, but I must separate them. They already had a frightful row earlier this morning." She hurried away, and he suddenly felt a little colder.

As the morning wore on, others from the party came to sit with him. At one point, Miss Church-Pratton chatted incessantly with him for half an hour. Miranda was speaking to Mrs. Peterson, the rector's wife, but Gerard finally managed to catch her eye. She smiled at him, and within a few minutes, Lady Wynwood joined him again. This time, Miss Church-Pratton remained only a minute before leaving.

"You are fortunate," Lady Wynwood said. "Sir Horace has become a rival for Miss Church-Pratton's hand."

"I am certain I can withstand the disappointment. Who is the gentleman?"

She nodded to an elderly man who had joined Mr. Solomon Drydale near one of the fires next to the lake. "He is a relative of Mrs. Barnes, and indecently wealthy. However, I assure you that you are much more handsome."

"The curse of a pretty face. Shall I have Mr. Drydale plant me a facer to break my nose?"

"*I* can do that for you." She grinned at him. "I am out of sorts with Sol. He mentioned to me that Sir Horace is a fine judge of horseflesh, so when I was introduced to him, I asked him about his stable. Did you know that he has *fifty-nine* horses?"

"That is a great many."

"Yes, especially when Sir Horace proceeded to recite the lineage of each and every one of them."

He laughed.

Lady Wynwood turned toward the lake before them. "What a lovely view you have here. '*The heavens declare the glory of God; and the firmament sheweth his handywork,*' indeed."

"I would not have expected the woman who speaks of muslin enhancements at a ball to be so well-versed in Scripture."

"Fashion foibles and a vulgar sense of humor do not preclude a sense of the spiritual. I do not find muslin enhancements unholy."

"Yes, ma'am, I see that."

"Do you? We are none of us saints, Gerard." Her light

brown eyes had turned golden in the sunlight. She absently touched the narrow streak of silver at her temple, barely visible against the blond hair mostly hidden by her bonnet. It appeared she did not notice she was doing it. "We would do well to always remember that, lest we become self-righteous and hypocritical. But by the grace of our Lord Jesus Christ, we are forgiven our sins, such as they are."

He felt suddenly as though he were on holy ground. Her words touched something in his soul that he did not quite understand. "None of us like to dwell on our sins, I think."

"Of course not, but I have come to appreciate a good confessional prayer. It is like giving my heart a good scrubbing. When I am here at Wintrell Hall, I pray in the chapel nearly every midday."

"I did not know that. Did you always do so?"

Her gaze became distant and burdened. "No. Only in the past ten years or so."

Down by the shore, Mrs. Hathaway waved frantically to them.

"Oh, there's Augusta waving to us to return. Gerard, I nearly forgot to mention that your mother had a message for you. She and your father left earlier and I am to take you back to the house in my carriage. Shall I assist you?"

His knee would pain him when he stood, and he had no wish to be helped anywhere. "No, I shall follow in a moment."

"Very well. Don't dawdle." But before she moved away, she said, "I am still speaking to your mother about Miranda. I believe she may be having a change of heart, although I am not yet certain."

He bowed as she left. The children had been called in from the ice, and the party was heading back to the house. Automatically, as he used to do when they were children, he began to count the heads of the young ones. Twenty-seven. Hadn't there been twenty-eight in total? How many children had arrived at the lake? Perhaps one of them had remained at the house, or returned earlier.

Gerard grasped his crutches and heaved himself up. Because he had been sitting for so long, his knee immediately responded with the pain of a thousand knife blades stabbing into it. He gritted his teeth and bowed his head, waiting for the wave to pass.

He caught Miranda's eye and signaled to her. As she approached, he asked, "How many children came to the lake?"

"Twenty-eight."

"A moment ago, I counted only twenty-seven."

She immediately frowned and stared down at the children, her lips moving silently. "You are correct. It is easier to count from this vantage point."

"Who is missing?"

"I do not see Paul, do you?"

He scanned the heads. Paul had been wearing a bright maroon cap. "No, I do not see him."

"I think I know where he is. He and the others made a snow fort in the woods earlier this morning." She gestured behind him, toward the tree line.

Alarm shot through him. "I will come with you."

She glanced at him suspiciously, but only said, "Come along, then." She tramped into the woods.

Although he had to hurry to catch up to her, he found

it a relief that she did not try to argue with him or treat him differently because of his injury. But this was Miranda, and she never responded in the way one might expect.

Then, when they were deep enough into the woods to have lost sight of the lake, they were attacked.

The men came from a different direction than the one he had been anticipating. Miranda was only two feet in front of him when one of the same men from the garden suddenly rushed at her, throwing a sack over her head. She shrieked but her voice was muffled by fabric caught in her mouth. The man tossed her over his shoulder.

Gerard swung his crutch and caught the man in the leg. He stumbled and dropped Miranda, who landed hard on the ground.

At that moment, the second man ran toward him. Gerard caught the dull gleam of the knife blade just in time to jerk backward. He quickly shifted his grip on the other crutch so that the wood was braced against his forearm and blocked the man's next swing with the knife.

Where was the other jaw of his trap—where was Michael?

But Gerard had no opportunity to look around as the knife stabbed toward him. He threaded the blade through the crutch and twisted. The knife flicked through the air, and the man looked at his empty hand in disbelief. Gerard slammed the other crutch into the man's nose, and he howled and jumped backward.

Gerard looked up in time to see Miranda shove her fingers into the first man's eyes, and he cried out, releasing his grip on her. She shoved at the sack still over her head.

At that moment, a third man moved from behind a tree and grabbed Miranda's attacker from behind. It was Michael.

"Miranda, run!" Gerard said.

She pulled the sack from her head and ran back towards the lake.

But Gerard's attacker lunged to follow her. Gerard tripped him with his crutch, but the man's leg pulled at it. Gerard staggered and pain stabbed through his knee. He fell to the ground with the other man, who kicked at him, but Gerard rolled out of the way.

Miranda's attacker pulled out a knife and slashed at Michael, who released him and leaped back. Then the attacker ran back into the woods.

The man on the ground with Gerard also jumped to his feet and followed his compatriot.

Michael ran after them.

Gerard shoved himself to his feet. His knee throbbed once, so painfully that his vision clouded briefly, then receded to a spiking ache. He reached out and grabbed one of his crutches from the ground, then hurried after them.

It was easier for him to maneuver through the narrow deer trails with only one crutch, but he did not move quickly enough. He could see movement ahead of him through the trees, and he followed the shadow.

But when he rounded a tree, he lost sight of the shadow. He stopped, his eyes scanning the dimness. No movement. A bird called feebly, as if reluctant to break the silent vanguard of old oaks. A scurrying to his right, but it sounded like a mouse.

Then, ahead of him, a shadow detached itself from behind a tree and approached him.

Gerard exhaled. "Lost them?"

"Sorry, old chap."

"You're a poor bodyguard, Cousin. I wondered if you'd received my message."

Gerard's cousin, Lieutenant Michael Coulton-Jones, wore a thoroughly disreputable costume in motley shades of dirt, slime, and moss on his worn clothes. Mud almost hid the grin across his handsome face. "I hid in a tree where I could see all the paths someone was likely to take in order to sneak up behind you on that bench, just as you told me to do. It is hardly my fault that I was thwarted by a dozen children creating a fort under the tree where I was hiding."

"Paul and his company, I suspect."

"Yes, the one giving orders was named Paul. I couldn't drop down and scare them half to death, and they were making such a rumpus that I suspect your attackers chose a more circuitous route on their way to relieve you of your life."

"Trapped by a gaggle of children? Embarrassing, Michael." Gerard sobered. "Did the children see the attackers? Did they harm them?"

"All the children left but Paul, who left a few minutes later. Then I heard a woman scream."

"That must have been Miranda. Michael, they were after her, not me."

"That sheds a different light upon it."

Behind them, someone called Gerard's name.

"I'll find you later," Michael said.

"I hope you find different clothing. You look like

something the hunting dogs vomited up."

Michael drew himself to his full height, which made his hideous clothes rain dirt upon the ground. "I'll have you know that I was perfectly concealed in the tree while wearing these clothes."

"I'm surprised the children didn't smell your presence."

The corner of Michael's mouth curled up. Then in the blink of an eye he was gone, disappearing behind the tree.

In the next moment, Gerard heard a soft tread behind him. He turned to see Mr. Drydale running toward him, appearing from behind a clump of trees.

"Gerard, are you harmed? Miranda said two men attacked you both."

"They ran. I was following, but I lost them."

"Were you speaking to someone?" Mr. Drydale's dark eyes regarded the tree, although his face was impassive.

"I spoke with a tenant who happened to be in the woods. Er ... I promised him I would not mention to Sir Cecil about his presence in an area popular with poachers."

Mr. Drydale's eyebrows rose. "I see. Did he see them?"

"He saw movement, but thought it was a deer. I am afraid they are out of our reach by now, sir."

Mr. Drydale accompanied Gerard to retrieve his other crutch and they returned to the lake together. Almost all the women and children had already gone back to the house with the servants and supplies, leaving only several of the menfolk, Lady Wynwood, Miranda, and Paul. Upon hearing about the attack and being assured that Gerard was unharmed, they all returned to the house in their carriages.

He rode with Mr. Drydale and Lady Wynwood, whose carriage was one of the last to reach the hall. Gerard's father and mother met him at the door to the house. He forestalled them by telling them, "I am well."

"Oh, Gerard, if only we had not left the lake so early," his mother moaned.

"How's the leg?" his father asked.

It had been feeling as though a hammer had been attempting to pound its way in, but he said, "No worse than before. I must change out of my wet things."

After Maddox had helped him into a dressing gown and left him seated before the fire, he was surprised by a knock at the door. Cecil, Mr. Belmoore, and Gerard's father were there.

His father and Mr. Belmoore seated themselves, but Cecil stood before the fireplace. His father's unhappy expression made Gerard tense.

"My boy, what a terrible thing to have happened," Mr. Belmoore said.

"I will find these men, I assure you," Gerard said. He hadn't the faintest idea what he would do, but surely sheer determination should count for something.

"We are concerned about you," Mr. Belmoore said.

"I am perfectly—"

"We are concerned about what you may have done to cause someone to want to harm you," Cecil said sharply.

"Cecil!" Mr. Belmoore said. "Good God, he's just been attacked."

"Probably by the same two men from the garden," Cecil retorted. "Are those men connected to that vagrant woman in the woods? Why are they after Gerard and Miranda? We are all thinking it, even if none of us speaks of it to the rest of the household."

Gerard should have been expecting this. His mother had mentioned something like this only a few days before. But he felt like a statue in an ice-covered garden. He had difficulty breathing. "I have done nothing of which I am ashamed. Nothing which would shame you or the family."

"I have no doubt of it." However, his father would not meet his eyes.

No, he was not a statue. He was a block of ice that had been shattered into razor-sharp shards.

He would not stand for this. He had faults enough, but he had never been dishonorable. How could they suspect that he'd been involved in anything that would draw such danger and unsavory characters to the Belmoore family home? The frustration made him shoot to his feet and limp to the fireplace. His knee was a ball of heat and pain, but his emotions were an ice storm.

"Gerard, you must sit," his father said.

Gerard ignored him. He would not tell them that the men had been after Miranda, for what would Cecil do to her then? Instead, Gerard would find these men and make them tell him why they were doing this. He would prove himself and Miranda innocent.

But he also knew that his relationship with the Belmoores had changed. He stared into the fire and felt as though something inside of him had withered and died.

Chapter Thirteen

December 29th

She was wearing his scarf.

Gerard made his way out through the portico on the south side of the house, placing the crutches carefully on the icy stones. It had snowed last night, a few inches, and the children were having a rousing snowball fight on the south lawn. Miranda sat on a bench at the edge of the flagstone terrace, and his red and black scarf around her neck was a splash of color on the white landscape beyond her.

She turned and saw him as he exited the house. Her face was pale, and for a moment she looked apprehensive. Then she gave a small smile that commanded the wind and waves of his anxiety to be still. The air sliced through his nose and lungs, but despite the cold, he reveled in the clean scent of freshly fallen snow, of firs and woodsmoke.

She rose and walked towards him. "You should be resting."

"It is the case of the pot and kettle brangling with

each other," he said.

"I do not brangle." Her eyes crinkled. "And I was not injured."

"You were attacked, the same as I." His voice was too forceful, and he took a breath before continuing, "It frightened me."

A whisper of emotion passed over her face. It reminded him of a child pressing her nose to the glass of a candy shop. Then it was gone, and she was the same calm, dependable Miranda.

"Come sit." She pointed to the bench. "I have swept the snow from it."

She walked beside him as he made his way to the edge of the flagstones. "Miranda," he said in a low voice, "you should not be sitting alone. It is not safe—those men were focused upon you."

She said nothing. She dipped her head so he could not see her face beyond the edge of her bonnet.

"Miranda, you cannot avoid this discussion."

Still she said nothing.

He sighed. "I will bring up the *other* topic of conversation you wish to avoid if you do not speak."

"Oh, for goodness' sake." She looked at him then, her cheeks pink.

It made him want to kiss her again.

However, he missed his chance, because she looked away again, hiding behind the edge of her bonnet. "Everyone is gossiping about the attack. I have been circumspect in what I have said about it, although I am not certain whether that is the wisest course."

Gerard remembered the tense conversation with Cecil, Mr. Belmoore, and his father. "It is. No one knows that the men specifically wanted you except for myself and, er ..."

"That man who helped me? Who was he?"

"It was my cousin, Michael. Have you never met him?"

"Perhaps when we were children, but not in the past several years. You said that you had sent for someone to help us—it was Michael?"

"Yes. I had gone to the skating party in hopes that the men would attack me. Michael was lying in wait to ambush them."

"Ah." She nodded. "That was a good plan."

"It was? It didn't work."

"It was still a good plan."

In the midst of the distant snowball fight, Ellie caught sight of her and Gerard and waved.

Miranda waved back. "I cannot avoid the children, but I did not wish to be near them, in case ..."

They had nearly reached the bench, but he stepped on a patch of ice and his foot slid out sideways, catching her ankle. The sudden pressure on the opposite crutch sent it skidding in the other direction. He had a view of wildly spinning sky, and then the hard smack of the stones beneath his back, the clatter of his falling crutches. Miranda also gave a little squeak and fell with him, her cloak and skirts tangled around his foot.

"Miranda, are you—"

She burst into laughter.

In the sound of her laugh, his crutches, the symbol of his weakness and the root of his bitterness, lost some of their evil. In the sound of her laugh, he was not a cripple, but a man lying tangled in the skirts of a beautiful woman on a beautiful winter day.

Hang her relations, who might see them from the windows of the house behind them. He wanted to cup her face and kiss her senseless.

He had fallen in love with her.

He might have fallen in love with her the moment she stepped into his family's coach. He remembered the rush when he'd seen her, the notion that she was linked to him. He had known her for most of his life, but he had fallen in love with her this past week as he had seen how she fit with him, like a key in a lock.

Her laughter had died to gasping breaths. "Come, Gerard, the ground is too cold."

Her words were too mundane for what he was feeling. And yet what could he say? Confess his love? Propose to her? He'd sound like a madman.

He was so much less than he had been. He was still uncomfortable with the thought of offering himself to any woman, but especially Miranda. He knew that she would accept him, she would willingly shoulder the burden of his care.

He did not wish to do that to her, to be yet another person who *needed* something from her.

They sat on the bench, and despite the pain in his leg, his body felt so much more alive than it had in months. Miranda had done this to him. Love had done this to him.

"Miranda—"

"Miranda!" The governess hurried toward her. "Paul is quite upset because Sally is wearing his mittens rather than her own. Would you fetch hers from the nursery and put Paul's mittens away?" She gave Miranda a set of blue mittens.

"Of course. If you'll excuse me, Gerard?" And then Miranda was gone, leaving only a whiff of lavender and lemon behind her.

Gerard sat there feeling nonplussed. What had he been about to say to her? What could he say? He was being a complete lackwit.

Well, that was nothing unusual.

*

After retrieving Sally's mittens, Miranda had reached the foot of the nursery wing stairs and started down the hallway to the main staircase when she saw the undermaid, Jean, looking around furtively with her hand on the latch to Cecil's bedroom. Jean froze when she saw Miranda.

"What are you doing?" Miranda demanded. Jean was not an upper-maid, nor was she Cecil's valet, so she should not be entering Cecil's room for any reason.

Jean's eyes were wide for a moment, then she affected an innocent expression. "Sir Cecil is in a snit because his grandfather's pistol is missing. I am helping to search for it." She smirked at Miranda.

"You are not."

"Are you calling me a liar?"

"I am." Miranda drew herself up. She was a poor relation now, but she was also a gentleman's daughter and had been the only daughter of a wealthy household. In her father's home, Jean would have been sacked for such belligerence to any guest.

Jean stood there stiffly, her hands clenching and unclenching at her sides. Then she gave Miranda a nasty smile. "What will you do about it? Will you have me turned out? Lady Belmoore won't listen to *you*."

"Let's find out, shall we?"

"Or p'raps you'll resort to other ways to get me sacked. I hear you're quite good at it." Jean whirled in a flurry of skirts and stalked away.

The hallway tilted. Miranda thrust out blindly for the wall, sagging against it. Her stomach heaved.

Jean knew. And there was only one way she could know. She'd been told.

The light dimmed, darkness threatening to cover her, but she fought it, dragging in deep breaths, willing her heartbeat to ease and slow.

She knew who was after her. And why.

Chapter Fourteen

Gerard almost didn't notice the footman. He wanted to say it was because he was distracted, but in reality, it was because Michael was that accomplished.

After Miranda left him, Gerard was too cold to remain out of doors and was seeking the comfort of his fire and perhaps a pot of tea with a splash of whiskey in it for good measure. However, the way to his bedroom was blocked by footmen leaving the music room, each carrying some chairs that had been stored there. They headed toward the drawing room, and Gerard guessed that the extra chairs were for the guests tonight. Felicity had planned a lavish dinner party for this evening.

A certain footman passed Gerard, his ill-fitting livery looking as though it had been made for someone else. At first, the man's face was that of a complete stranger. Then suddenly the servant turned a glass-green eye toward him and winked.

Gerard ground his teeth.

He headed slowly down the hallway, past the music room and toward his bedroom. He paused at his door, waiting.

The butler stood supervising while the footmen silently wove around him. The footman in question exited the drawing room, returning to the music room for more chairs, but Gerard made certain to send him a pointed glare before going into his bedroom. Gerard settled in front of the fireplace and waited.

In a few moments, there was a scratch at the door. "Come," he bellowed.

"You're cross as a bear," Michael said as he entered the room, closing the door behind him. He had suddenly become Michael again, rather than the strange servant Gerard had first seen.

"Why are you in that livery?" Gerard demanded.

Michael tried to look innocent as he tugged at his sleeves. "I should think it obvious. And you will surely get me sacked, wanting to speak to me when I should be working."

"It is too risky for you to insinuate yourself as one of the servants," Gerard said. "We discussed this when you first arrived."

"I cannot protect you if I continue in my guise as a peddler in the village," Michael said.

"My father—your uncle—may recognize you, you fool."

Michael gave him a level look. "*You* did not. And you are forgetting, Cousin, that day in France. I can fool him, I assure you."

Gerard's ire drained out of him.

Two years ago, Gerard had led a crew on shore to capture some Frenchmen who were resupplying their ship from a French village. There was a skirmish and some of the peasants had been captured along with the seamen.

Gerard had stared his cousin in the face and not recognized him until hours later, when the French peasant managed to unobtrusively whisper to him with Michael's voice. He had confessed that he was on assignment for the Foreign Office and had asked Gerard to find a way to free him. There was apparently more to Michael's duties than simply being one of Wellington's junior officers.

After the woman's attack on Christmas Eve, Gerard had written to Michael, whom he knew was on leave at home this Christmas, to ask for his help in investigating the woman. Michael had gone so far as to blacken his hair, and when posing as a peddler, the dirt hid his features. Now, he had no dirt but he had done something to make his face appear sallow, and when Gerard had seen him carrying chairs, his gait and posture had been completely different from his normal upright carriage.

Michael gave his carefree smile. "Besides, no one notices servants."

Gerard admitted he was probably correct.

Michael continued, "The peddler guise was useful when I became drinking partners with nearly every man in the local tavern, looking for any local family with a connection to you or Miranda. But after the attack yesterday, I thought it would be better to be here to protect her. And to ensure the safety of my ungrateful relative, of course."

"I am not ungrateful," Gerard growled. "I am concerned about you."

"I am touched by your solicitude." Michael gave a

short bow. “It is mutual. Especially when you insist on attempting to lure the men out of hiding by dangling yourself as bait.”

“I cannot sit here in safety and do nothing. Surely you understand that.”

Michael’s eyes were serious as they rested upon him. “Yes, I do.”

A sudden frantic knocking at the door made them both turn. In an instant, Michael’s face underwent an astounding transformation. He altered the muscles of his jaw and lips, relaxing some and tightening others, and suddenly his chin seemed weaker, his eyes half-lidded, and in combination with the slouch of his shoulders and the makeup on his face, he hardly looked like himself. He shuffled to the door to answer it.

Miranda started in surprise at the sight of him, but her eyes slid over him to Gerard. Her face had turned so pale that her skin was translucent.

“Miranda, what’s wrong?” He rose to his feet, ignoring the protest from his knee.

She gulped and glanced at Michael.

“Hurry, come inside,” Gerard said.

Miranda did not even hesitate at the impropriety and slipped into his bedroom. Michael closed the door behind her and relaxed his facial muscles again, which made her squeak in surprise.

“Miranda, may I introduce my cousin, Lieutenant Michael Coulton-Jones. Miss Miranda Belmoore.”

“Charmed.” Michael bowed over her hand and gave one of the dashing smiles that caused every woman he’d ever known to swoon at his feet.

Gerard scowled at him. However, he was gratified

when Miranda pulled her hand from his quickly and turned toward Gerard.

But now that she was in private with him, she seemed anxious and nervous. "Gerard, you should sit. And not because of your knee."

"What is it?" He sank gratefully back into the sofa while she settled on a chair.

"I ..." She squeezed her eyes shut as if trying to block out a horrible memory. "I know who wants to kill me."

"Who?"

She pressed her fist to her mouth, and he saw she was trembling. He reached for her, no matter that Michael stood by the fire with an interested expression on his face, and held her hand in his own.

The eyes she raised to his were tortured. "Gerard, it is all my fault."

"Miranda—"

"Do you remember what I told you about my parents? They hired a new nursery maid when I was six years old, but they were unconcerned with the goings on in the nursery. Harriet ..." She swallowed. "Harriet was cruel and told my parents that I was clumsy." She absently ran her hand over her forearm. "And so my parents never questioned the bruises."

A rage built up in his chest, tightening every muscle in his body. He had to concentrate to keep from crushing her hand. He focused on the delicate bones of her fingers, so fragile next to his. He could protect her now. He *would* protect her now from anyone who would harm her, because he loved her.

"It went on for two years," Miranda said. "Then one day I found my mother's diamond bracelet under a bush in the garden. She had put the house in an uproar because she'd lost the bracelet two or three nights before at a dinner party she'd given. The bracelet must have slipped off when she went walking in the gardens after dinner. But instead of returning it, I hid the bracelet in Harriet's dresser. On Harriet's day off, one of the under-maids watched me, so I casually mentioned a pretty bracelet I'd seen Harriet wearing. It took very little encouragement to get the maid to look through Harriet's things and find my mother's bracelet. Harriet was sacked immediately and the maid promoted to an upper-maid."

"It's Harriet doing this?" Michael asked. Gerard had nearly forgotten he was there. "After all these years?"

"No one else in the neighborhood would hire her," Miranda said. "She was forced to go to London to find work, but fell on hard times. I heard that she had died, in a ... brothel."

Gerard saw the guilt in her expression. "You were only eight years old."

"I was old enough to know it would be hard for her to find another situation once she'd been accused of theft," Miranda said. "And later I understood what had happened to her in London. But at the time, all I felt was relief that she was gone." Her fingers clenched hard in his palm.

"You never saw the woman in the woods," Gerard said. "You can't know it's Harriet."

"Jean, one of the maids, alluded to how I could have her sacked," Miranda said. "She couldn't know unless Harriet had told her. No one else knew that I had hidden that bracelet among Harriet's things in order to get her sacked. She must have used Jean to open the garden gate so those two men could attack us."

"No, she couldn't have known the two of you would walk outside that night," Michael said.

"Perhaps they would have entered the house and waited for you," Gerard said grimly.

"It seems incredible that Harriet happened to find you," Michael said. "And those two men—she must have hired them. There is something about this that seems odd."

"I considered leaving Wintrell Hall," Miranda said in a low voice.

Gerard's heart twisted once, hard. "There is nowhere you could go. You would be like Harriet."

"It would draw her away from all of you."

"This is not some penance you must pay," he said fiercely.

"We can use this to our advantage," Michael said. "Set a trap. We nearly had them at the skating party."

"I won't put Miranda in danger," Gerard told his cousin.

"She wouldn't be. I will need to think on this."

"We will both think on this. In the meantime, Miranda, remain close to the house and go nowhere alone. Since Michael is now one of the servants, he can help watch over you."

Michael gave him a smug smile. "I told you it would be useful for me to be here."

Gerard gave him a dark look. "You are useful only if you are not caught out."

Chapter Fifteen

The bell to dress for dinner had already rung, but something drew Laura, Lady Wynwood, past her bedroom and up the stairs to an older section of the house. She followed a winding route she remembered well from her childhood, taking her from staircase to hallway to staircase, always climbing upward. At the top of the last narrow set of stairs, she wrestled with the door, but it eventually flung open to the pressure of her shoulder against it, and she was out on the rooftop of Wintrell Hall.

The brick cupola, slit with glass to let light fall into the great front hall far below, was flanked by two small turrets, one containing the door out of which she stepped. The wind whistled harder at this height, but she'd brought her fur-edged cloak, and the fresh bite of the cold air made her feel awake and alive.

A brick parapet ringed the cupola, and she passed through an opening to walk around and view the countryside. She could see the tracks in the snow on the front lawn where the children had had a snowball fight this morning, while beyond the trees glistened with the snow and ice dripping from their branches. Farther out, the pasturelands lay in squares and rectangles, broken by hedgerows and the dark line of the river. The setting sun was just starting to turn the sky rosy and golden.

Her thoughts wandered. The cold stung her cheeks but the view was too beautiful to leave it, the peace too delicious to want to stop soaking in it.

But then the sound of the door opening made her turn, and Miranda stepped out onto the roof.

Her eyes—oh, her eyes were like those of the dead.

She made as if to leave, but Laura held out her hand. "Come enjoy the view with me."

Miranda hesitated for so long, Laura was not certain she would join her. But then she stepped through the opening in the parapet on slow feet and came to stand beside her.

"I did not mean to interrupt you," Miranda said.

"You did not, my dear."

"The first bell has rung."

"Yes, I know, but ..." Laura took a deep breath. "It is all your fault."

"Mine?" Her green eyes were hazel in the rose-orange light.

"You are so restful, Miranda, and I ... I am like Gerard, always wanting to do something. And so I am here, seeking peace, seeking the Lord."

Miranda's gaze flicked away.

"Is that why you are here?" Laura asked.

Miranda's mouth opened, searching for the words to say. "I don't know," she finally said. Her jaw worked. It seemed to Laura that Miranda's emotions were crawling under her skin and she was struggling to keep them in.

Laura would have asked, but something almost like a physical touch stayed her voice. So instead, she turned to drink in the view and remained silent.

Laura worried that Miranda would simply return inside, but she stood there beside her for several long minutes.

"Coming up here reminds me of how small I am," Miranda said.

"Yes, '*What is man, that thou art mindful of him? or the son of man, that thou visitest him?*' Hebrews."

Miranda blinked. "That's in the Bible?"

"Of course, my dear. Why does that surprise you?"

She frowned. Her gaze remained on the view, but Laura could tell that she didn't see it. "I ... I never thought God would be mindful of me."

"Whyever not? He created you. He loves you more deeply than any parent ever could."

Miranda's jaw grew hard, and her eyes grew sad. "That would not be difficult. I never mattered to them."

Laura had a sudden memory of a summer day here at Wintrell Hall, and Miranda's mother complaining to her and Augusta about how, during the Season in London, they had not been able to find a man to take Miranda off their hands.

"My dear." Laura turned Miranda to face her. "If you believe nothing else I tell you, believe this. You matter to God, a great deal, and He loves you exactly the way He made you."

She gave a little shake of the head. "Why would God see someone like me?"

"Come, I will tell you a story." Laura threw her arm around Miranda and led her around the cupola. "There was a slave who was mistreated by her mistress, so she ran away. But God saw her in the wilderness and spoke to her."

Miranda's brow wrinkled, but she said nothing.

Laura continued, "People in those days liked naming things, so she gave God another name. She called him, *Thou God seest me.*"

By now, they had reached the other side of the cupola. In the dome, the rectangular panels of glass had circular designs within them, and the setting sun shone through a circle, looking a bit like an eye. Laura stopped. "She was only a slave, but He *saw* her, Miranda."

Miranda looked at the orange light for a few seconds, but then turned her face away. Laura saw her expression and was haunted by it, because it was despair.

"*I* see you, Miranda," Laura said. "And I have to believe God will find a way for you out of these troubles."

"Yes," Miranda said, but absently. "I must go." She headed toward the turret door, but then she suddenly turned and embraced Laura in a fierce hug.

She was gone in a moment, passing through the door and down the narrow staircase.

Laura stood there, her heart throbbing hard and slow. Miranda's hug had almost seemed like good-bye.

Chapter Sixteen

December 30th

Gerard had wearied of staring at his bedroom walls while submitting to another poultice, so after Maddox had removed it, he went to stretch his legs.

The drawing room was stuffed, like a meat pie, but with chattering young women discussing their gowns for the New Year's Eve dinner party the next evening. Gerard sneaked past the doorway and headed instead to the music room, where he heard the laughter of children.

For most of the year, the ballroom at Wintrell Hall served as the music room on one side, and store-room on the other half, separated by some painted folding screens. He didn't realize until he entered the room that he had hoped to see Miranda there, but it was the governess at the pianoforte while the girls still in the schoolroom were learning the steps of a dance. Gerard was surprised to see his mother teaching them, correcting footwork and handclasps, her face alight with laughter. She smiled when she spotted her son in the open doorway.

"Oh, good," his mother said, "now Gerard can play so Miss Teel can help teach the girls."

"I?" He was embarrassed at how his voice squeaked. "Madam, I have not played the pianoforte in *years*—"

"Oh, you needn't give a perfect performance. We merely need a light little air so the girls can learn the steps. And the slower you play, the better."

Trapped, he made his way to the instrument, perhaps taking longer than he might have otherwise with his crutches. He seated himself and rested the crutches against a nearby chair. Miss Teel, the governess, had been playing a fairly simple repeating melody, and he realized he could dance (ha ha) his way around the more difficult passages.

He began, slowly and with absolutely horrible fingering, slamming chords about like a ship on stormy seas. But after struggling through the melody twice, he eventually found his sea legs and was able to play only half as slowly as Miss Teel had been playing. He even found himself enjoying watching the girls whirl about, giggling at their own mistakes.

The door to the music room opened, and Miranda appeared. Her eye caught Gerard's. They glowed for a moment, then she looked away.

He had not had a moment alone with her, or at least, a time long enough to pluck up his courage to say what he wished to say. He had never felt so awkward with her before, after all the years they had known each other.

She had also never before been so unguarded. He could see the pain and guilt in her eyes, the unease. It had seemed unsuitable for him to speak of his feelings.

So he had done what he could do. He had been a

comforting presence when she desired it. Indeed, he could not remember a time he had ever been so patient.

"The bell to dress for dinner is about to ring," Miranda said. "It is time for the girls to prepare for their supper in the nursery."

Cecil's middle daughter, Julia, gave her younger sister an exuberant swing around, her frothy laughter filling the echoing room.

The abused sister, Constance, scowled at her. "*Why* is Julia allowed to join the adults at table and not me? I'm only two years younger." The whining voice made it apparent this was an argument she'd already made today, probably several times.

"Because your mother needs an even number at table tonight," Gerard's mother said. "And since the men outnumber the ladies by one, I convinced your mother to allow Julia to join us."

"It's not fair," Constance complained as Miranda led her out of the music room.

"Miranda," his mother called, "you received my message? I can't think how Felicity forgot to include you."

"Yes, Mrs. Foremont," Miranda said. "Thank you." She and the governess left with the girls without looking at Gerard again, and he felt strangely let down.

"Thank you, Gerard." His mother sat beside him. "You played wonderfully."

"Thank you." He cleared his throat. "Mother, about Miranda ..."

"Yes, I was surprised when I discovered this morning that Miranda had not been included among the guests for tonight. It is only a small dinner party, and Felicity said Miranda would not mind since there were already even numbers, but I felt that would be insulting to her. After all, she is a poor relation, not a servant."

"That may not be clear in Felicity's mind."

"I pointed out that including both Miranda and Julia would ensure a gentleman for every lady, and it would also be good practice for Julia. She does not come out for another year, but little James Barnes is attending tonight."

"He is up from Oxford so he is little no longer," Gerard said, laughing.

"Well, he would otherwise be the youngest guest. He will be able to talk to Julia. And Miranda will be there to smooth over any *faux pas*. I simply did not feel comfortable excluding her."

He hadn't expected this kindness from his mother, considering her resistance in allowing Miranda to accompany Ellie. He realized that now it would not matter if she agreed or not, because he intended to marry Miranda. Er ... as soon as he asked her, that is. "Miranda is too often overlooked."

His mother looked down at her hands, fidgeting in her lap. "I have been most impressed with Miranda these past few days. She has been very patient in caring for you, spending time with you. More patient than I," she added in a low voice.

"Mother, you are very patient. You nursed me when I returned home from the hospital."

"But lately, I have had a rather short temper. And Miranda's kindness made me feel quite ashamed." She reached over to touch his hand. "I have been selfish. I wanted you to be completely healed in the shortest time possible, and I pray I have not pushed you to exertions that may have injured you."

"No, of course not, Mother."

"These attacks have made me realize that you are not as healed as I had wanted you to be, and that was very wrong of me." She squeezed his hand.

The bell rang.

"Come, Mother, we must dress for dinner." Gerard rose to his feet. His knee ached, and he grimaced as he rubbed at it. "Do not dare to coddle me, madam," he said before she could speak.

She smiled ruefully but only said, "I shall see you at dinner."

Tonight's dinner was an intimate gathering compared to the lavish New Year's Eve dinner party that would occur the following night, but the wine flowed freely, and the talk around the table was bright and sparkling.

Again, Miranda was seated far down the table from Gerard, on one side of James Barnes while Julia sat next to him. However, the two young people seemed to be in animated conversation and oblivious to their other dinner partners.

At one point, Miranda caught Gerard's eye. He glanced at the chattering pair, then back to her, and she smiled, sharing his silent amusement.

She looked beautiful, again in her green dress. He wanted to spend as much time with her as he wished. He wanted the shadow of Harriet's revenge to be lifted from her eyes.

He would speak to her soon—tonight or tomorrow. He did not think she would refuse him. He did not want to contemplate what he would feel if she did so.

Presently, Felicity rose to lead the women out of the dining room and into the drawing room. The men settled around the table and the servants began to serve brandy and cigars. However, Cecil, mindful of his wife, would not allow the men to linger overlong before joining the ladies in the drawing room.

As had happened yesterday, Michael, posing as a footman, had managed not to serve Gerard's father at dinner. However, now he poured brandy for the men, and Mr. Foremont did not notice him at all. Gerard did not realize he had been holding his breath until he released it.

Mr. Barnes, an avid angler, had been fishing only yesterday in the river that ran past his home and Wintrell Hall. He became so animated in his story that he began waving his arms to describe the fish he had caught, and the movement knocked into a young footman pouring more brandy into his glass. The young man stumbled backward, but Michael quickly reached out to steady the lad while at the same time preventing the decanter from crashing to the floor.

It all happened in a moment, but something in Michael's movements made Mr. Foremont's brows knit. For that second, Michael's disguise had faltered. He had immediately melted back into the unobtrusive servant, but now Gerard's father stared hard at the footman as he resumed his duties.

"Michael?" Gerard's father said.

Thankfully, Michael did not so much as flinch, nor did he respond to his name.

Sitting on his father's right, Gerard quickly said, "He has the look of a Coulton-Jones, does he not, sir? I thought as much when I saw him earlier today, so I made a point of speaking to him. However, he is not a relation, even distantly."

His father relaxed back into his seat. "He looks a bit like Michael."

"I have had a letter from Michael only yesterday," Gerard said. "He is enjoying Christmastide with his extended family, although the younger cousins are rather merciless in snowball fights."

"Michael wrote to you?"

"I wrote to him weeks ago asking if he would be interested in one of my hunters." Gerard sighed. "Since he is Michael, he waited until this week to respond."

His father chuckled and turned to Mr. Drydale, sitting on his left. "Did you hear that Cecil has unearthed his grandfather's pistol? It had fallen behind a desk drawer, of all places."

Mr. Drydale seemed to be looking in Michael's direction, also, but he turned his attention to Gerard's father. "Indeed, sir, he showed it to me yesterday. It must have taken him a great while to clean and repair it."

The men did not remain long in the dining room and soon rose to head to the drawing room. However, Mr. Drydale laid an arm along Gerard's shoulder. "A word, Captain Foremont, if you please."

"Of course, sir."

"Shall we go into the library? We may be assured of more privacy there."

Mr. Drydale's demeanor was calm and affable, but there was a hardness in his hazel eyes that made the muscles tighten at the base of Gerard's skull. He reined in his curiosity and followed the older man to the library, thumping along on his crutches.

As soon as the door was closed behind them, Mr. Drydale shoved Gerard hard against the wall, his forearm slicing his throat.

Gerard was the same height as Mr. Drydale, but thrown off his guard, he was tossed about like a limp puppet. His crutches clattered to the floor.

"I saw that man with you in the wood," Mr. Drydale bit out. "I saw him a day earlier in the local tavern, posing as a peddler. Now I see him here as a footman and you claim to have spoken to him again. What game are you playing, Captain?"

"He is my cousin, Lieutenant Michael Coulton-Jones," Gerard said in a tight voice. "He was helping me to investigate the attackers, since anyone connected with them is unlikely to speak candidly to me."

Mr. Drydale seemed nonplussed by that confession. He dropped his arm, and Gerard rubbed his neck, which still burned despite the fact that the pressure against his windpipe had been released.

"Who is he?" Mr. Drydale said.

"He is my cousin," Gerard repeated, but Mr. Drydale cut him off with an impatient hand.

"He is not simply your cousin. I did not recognize him as the man in the woods until he caught that decanter. Only then did I also recognize him as the peddler who defended a barmaid from a belligerent customer in the village tavern."

Gerard faced the older man, his jaw working. "I cannot say more than that he is my cousin, sir."

Mr. Drydale regarded him steadily for a moment, then

gave a self-deprecating half-smile, which brought out a dimple in his cheek and made him look years younger. "No, you cannot. I should have realized that. I would hazard a guess that you saw him on the continent at some point."

Gerard fought to keep his face impassive.

Mr. Drydale bowed to him. "Forgive me, Captain."

Gerard nodded stiffly.

"And should you need my assistance," Mr. Drydale said, "I am at your service. I, too, understand about certain things of which we cannot speak."

Gerard did not know how to respond, so he simply bowed in return, his mind whirling. Mr. Drydale came from an old, highly respectable family and he had heard someone say that he had served in the army in his youth. But this was an entirely unexpected revelation.

Mr. Drydale opened the library door, but paused to add, "If you trust Lady Wynwood, you may trust me, Captain." He left the room.

Gerard gathered his fallen crutches, feeling as though he had awakened from a dream. This Christmastide had revealed hidden depths to people he thought he knew well—Lady Wynwood's spiritual depth and maturity, Mr. Drydale's hinted past, and most especially, Miranda's inner peace and how it influenced him so strongly. But if he were honest with himself, there were many things about Miranda that he had discovered influenced him strongly—her quick wit, her sense of humor, and the loveliness that he had not noticed until meeting her eyes that day she climbed into their coach.

But when he entered the drawing room, Miranda was nowhere to be found. He could go to the nursery to see her, but did not want to embarrass her by seeking her out.

Tomorrow. He would settle all this tomorrow.

Chapter Seventeen

December 31st

The children were being positively horrid. Miranda, Miss Teel, and the nursery maids who worked for the other Belmoore families were quite prepared to begin stringing them up by their toes.

So Miranda suggested a game of Hide and Seek in the Lower Ornamental Garden. Miss Teel was amenable, but the nursery maids objected since they did not wish to trouble themselves to bundle up the children for the outdoors. However, the children were enthusiastic about the idea, and Miranda remarked that they would be entertaining themselves in such a way as to require very little supervision, since the garden was walled, so the maids were at last persuaded.

Wintrell Hall had two large walled gardens, the Upper and Lower Ornamental Gardens. They were accessed by a gate at the bottom of the Lower Garden. The Upper Garden was smaller and connected to the Lower Garden by a stone arch in the wall separating the two.

The Lower Garden had more hiding places for the

children, and Miss Teel and the two nursery maids sat at the gate to ensure that none of the children wandered out of their sight. Miranda walked up the winding paths to the archway.

The Upper Garden was bleak at this time of year, its bare trees covered in snow and the gravel walks lined only by twiggy bushes. It matched her low spirits, and she sat on a frozen stone bench along the wall, staring at the empty space. In the spring, it would be a riot of flowers, but today it lay sleeping.

The shrieks and laughter of the children drifted to her over the high stone wall and through the open archway, echoing oddly on the ice-covered stones. The sharp air bit into her nose and lungs, but the pain was somehow comforting.

One desperate act twenty years ago was at last reaping a bitter harvest. She could blame no one but herself.

She was so afraid.

"Oh, God." The cry escaped her lips, but the soft sound fell like wet snow. Cousin Laura was so assured of the presence of the Lord, but Miranda was alone in the garden. In her life, she had never felt that the Lord had been close to her—now was no different. Perhaps only people like Cousin Laura were invited into that type of fellowship with the Almighty.

And now that Gerard's mother appeared to be having a change of heart about her, it would be to no purpose if they did not stop Harriet. Ah, her timing was ever inconvenient.

Then came a soft, rhythmic sound. Man's boots and a pair of crutches crunching on the gravel paths. Coming closer.

Her heart raced with wild fear, with wild joy. Her body grew more and more taut as the sound drew near.

Gerard strode through the archway into the Upper Garden. When his gaze found hers, she could not have moved, like the lichen-covered marble statues in the corners of the garden.

She would never have expected the flame that lit his eyes when he saw her.

"Miranda." His voice tethered her to him, like a ship at anchor.

He came closer to her, moving carefully over the gravel walk until he stood before her, closer than she should have allowed. She realized too late that she should have moved toward him rather than the other way around. With the bench and the garden wall behind her, she felt as though he surrounded her.

"Are you hiding from the children?" he asked.

"In a sense."

He sat next to her on the bench, although he seemed closer than he ought to be. Certainly there was ample space on his other side, yet his shoulder brushed hers, his boot tangled in her cloak.

He most likely had a plan he had concocted with his cousin, Lieutenant Coulton-Jones. Something that would place all of them in danger. Or perhaps he had changed his mind and would not help her. He had come to his senses and decided she was more trouble than she was worth.

"Miranda," he said, staring ahead of him, "you do realize that you've been staring at a bush that looks like a gigantic turd?"

She choked, then laughed, her stomach tightening as she howled. "Gerard!"

"You looked so extremely serious," he said. "I thought I would try to lighten your mood." He swept his hand towards the offending bush. "And it truly does look like it. Cecil's gardener certainly has a sense of humor."

She hiccoughed, then snorted, then hiccoughed again.

"You're not choking, are you?" He glanced sideways at her.

"It would be your fault if I were."

"At least now you look less frightened."

"I am still frightened, Gerard."

"You are never frightened. Which is why I have a very dangerous proposition for you."

His words were serious and yet his tone was light. It confused her. "What is it?"

He turned to face her, and took her hands in his. Through their gloves she felt his warmth.

"Miranda, will you marry me?"

More than his question, the look in Gerard's eyes made her tremble. His eyes were shining amber flames and she was the moth, drawn towards them.

She had never allowed herself to dream of this moment, this question. Dreaming of it would have made her life all the more bleak. And now that he had asked it, with both of them sitting on an icy stone bench, she didn't know what to think, what to feel.

Why would he say such a thing to her? Surely he wasn't serious. He was simply being gallant and would regret his hasty words in a moment.

She swallowed and closed her eyes, shutting out that expression on his face that looked like love. When she opened her eyes, her calmness slid over her like a shroud. "Gerard, why should I do that?"

"I will do all I can to protect you. I will not leave you alone."

She had been alone, it seemed, for most of her life. Her parents had not even liked her, she suspected. She had not belonged to the set of people she'd met in London during her Season.

She knew Gerard was true to his word, he would not leave her alone. For a moment, she wanted to take hold of that, to have someone who was hers. She would be free of Harriet, of Cecil and Felicity.

But this new potential threat to her life enabled her to draw back. No, she would not marry him and expose him to the same threat. She turned her face away, her skin feeling like marble, her eyes downcast. "It is dangerous and foolhardy, Gerard."

"I don't care."

"I will not marry you for that reason." This was a terrible dream. It must be. She had loved him for so long, and yet now in this moment that she had never expected would happen to her, she was refusing him because she loved him. Because she couldn't bring this menace into his life. And so she lied to him. "I will not marry without love."

She thought that would silence him. He would assume she was a silly, romantical girl. But then the last words she expected tumbled out of his mouth.

"Miranda, I've fallen in love with you."

She looked at him, and her mind became a blank. She saw only his eyes, his beautiful eyes, intent upon her face. She wanted to tell him the truth. She wanted to see his smile, hear his laughter, find joy in his arms.

It was too hard to take that step. Men like him did not love women like her. She had to make him see that his emotions were only fleeting, a mad dream from which he would wake. She gave a short laugh, tinged with both sadness and incredulity. "In a week?"

Hurt flinched across his face, and she regretted her laugh and her words.

"You cannot tell me that I do not feel as I do," he said.

Her jaw set. "I will not allow you to make such a bad bargain."

His jaw set, as well. She had seen this stubbornness in him, but never directed at herself. "Why is it such a bad bargain if I am in love with you?"

Love. He kept saying the word, as if he meant it. He couldn't mean it. She had to convince him. Or perhaps ... she was trying to convince herself.

She took a deep breath, then faced him squarely. "Because I do not love you, Gerard."

Her hands shook as she said it, so she pulled them from his grasp and clamped them together, feeling her finger bones creak. But she had spent a lifetime perfecting this mask of calm—no, not a mask, a shield. She admitted it. But now, she was shielding him from herself.

He looked disbelieving, but in the face of her steady gaze, his skepticism began to crack, revealing ... pain, held at bay only by some inner strength. She recognized it. She'd felt it often enough when her parents had said something particularly denigrating, when Felicity's tongue ran sharp.

And she'd done it to Gerard.

"I ... I am sorry, that was too blunt," she said.

Gerard didn't respond, but his eyes spoke for him—he did not want to believe her, he could not believe that he would feel this way if she did not feel the same.

She did feel the same. She loved him. But she was in a walled garden of her own making, and she held the key. And she was too weak to unlock the gate and step outside.

She wanted to believe that she could be vulnerable, that she could learn to trust. But she had been this way for too long. It was too frightening to step out. There was that part of her that was perhaps too broken.

Miranda rose to her feet. She wanted to appear practical, unfeeling—but she gnawed nervously on her bottom lip and she could not meet his eyes.

He gathered his crutches and stood before her, a numb expression on his face.

Miranda stared at her feet. "I am sorry, Gerard. I am grateful for the honor of your proposal, but I cannot marry you."

She turned away to hurry back to the children.

Behind her, she thought she heard him growl, "I do not want your gratitude."

Then his hand captured her elbow. Not hard, but firmly enough to detain her. She turned back to demand that he release her.

His crutches clattered to the ground, and then his arms were around her, pulling her tight against his body. He kissed her, his lips firm and sensual.

Then she wrapped her arms around his neck, pulling his head down. Blood pulsed fast and hard in her ears, and she kissed him with all that her heart had to give to him.

His tongue touched her lips and she opened for him. His hand tightened on her waist, her back, and she pressed herself against him.

It was glorious. And for a moment, the Upper Garden was in full bloom.

He pulled away from her, breathing hard. His eyes were amber fires, and the love she saw in them made her want to weep.

Her breath was coming in soft gasps, but when she gently pushed at him and his arms loosened about her, she still couldn't seem to draw air into her lungs.

"Miranda, you lied to me." Fierce delight shone in his smile. "You do love me."

"I did not lie." She pushed away from him, slithering around him to walk a few feet away.

He took only one limping step toward her. "You cannot lie your way through this. I *felt* it."

She turned her back to him. He *had* felt it.

"Miranda, you must marry me."

"I do not want to marry you." Because she loved him, she also knew the most painful way to hurt him. "You say you can protect me, but we both know that a *cripple* cannot do so."

There was no sound behind her. She could not turn around to see his face, so she hurried out of the garden without looking back. Upon walking through the arch into the Lower Garden, she spotted a little boy hiding behind a manicured bush. Which admittedly looked like a gigantic turd.

"I see you, Paul!" She ran to him, arms outstretched

as though to tickle him to death.

He ran from her, screaming with laughter.

She played with the children for another half hour, but Gerard did not appear. When she, Miss Teel, and the nursery maids gathered the children and marched them back to the house for tea, he still had not departed from the bleak Upper Garden.

Chapter Eighteen

Gerard made his way blindly down the corridors. He knew Miranda could not have meant the callous words she had flung at him. She was not indifferent to him. She had given herself away with that kiss.

She would have refused him in order to keep him safe. The thought warmed through the cold that had seeped into his limbs. So she must have lied to him.

If she had lied, she was uncomfortably good at it. She had looked him in the eye to tell him she did not love him.

Why would she refuse him? He could offer her everything she did not have. He could protect her.

Unless, he realized bitterly, she truly did doubt his broken body's ability to protect her from anything.

No, he knew she had lied to him about that, too.

He knew where he wanted to go. He made his way deeper into the bowels of the house, searching out the older section. The carpets were older, smelling of long winters, and wall-hangings flanked the corridors like medieval squires.

At last he stood before the wooden door to the family

chapel. It was strangely shorter and narrower than he remembered, but the wood was still deeply grained, darkened with age and woodsmoke, studded with iron.

He pushed open the door, which gave a mighty creak. Colored light from the narrow stained-glass window over the altar dazzled his eyes, and it took him a moment to adjust to the darkness of the interior. Four pillars stood at attention, spreading outward at the top into the delicately vaulted ceiling. The wooden pews seemed almost crushed into the rest of the floor space since it was not a pretentiously grand chapel, being small and only modestly airy.

And near the front, Lady Wynwood turned to look at him. As soon as he saw her, he knew he needed her, even though he had not been able to articulate it to himself. He had come here to find her.

She rose and came to him, taking his hands in hers. "My dear boy, come and sit."

He sat with her in the front pew, resting his crutches against it. But now that he was here, he could not speak. The quiet of the chapel seeped into his bones, but instead of calming him, it only made him feel more helpless and vulnerable.

Lady Wynwood let him sit for several minutes before she spoke. "Won't you unburden yourself to me?"

"There is too much. It has shown me that I am less of a man because of it."

"Surely not, Gerard."

"What purpose has this served?" He gripped his knee, and pain shot down his leg. "Was I too proud? Was I in need of humbling? Did I do something that required judgment?"

"The Lord does not punish in that way."

"But He allowed this to happen." And therein lay the root of his problems. Because of his injury, he had not been able to protect Miranda as he would have had he been whole. He squeezed harder, sending pain spiking up his thigh.

Lady Wynwood gave him a frank look. "We think that there is a reason for everything. But the truth is that there are many reasons for everything." She laid her hand over his, smoothing the taut knuckles. "Your knee has brought you home to your parents, to a new chapter in your life."

Miranda had said much the same. "But this is not the chapter I wanted. Not so soon. I want to know why God has done this to me."

Her face had become drawn, and there was a hollowness and a horror behind her eyes that he had never seen before. "That is a trail that doubles back upon itself, and then doubles again."

He shot to his feet and limped to the altar. Dust coated the brocade cloth covering it.

"For me," she said from behind him, "anger is not a fire. It has been like drowning, a constant thrashing about, a constant questioning, 'Why me?' until it utterly exhausts me."

Perhaps she was right. He had lived with this bitterness for so many months that now he didn't know how to live without it, how to release this tightness in his soul.

"What would you suggest I do?" His voice was harsh. "Pray? Give alms to the poor?"

"Be still," she said simply.

He turned to look at her. She had a calmness of expression that reminded him of Miranda, but the weight of her gaze spoke of past pain, of hard lessons learned.

He swung back to the altar, his fingers wrinkling the cloth. "Since coming ashore, I have not been able to be still. I had more rest when I was on board ship, in the midst of a war."

"War has not followed you home, Gerard. There are different ways to fight the battles on land."

"What use is God when He takes away a man's career and leaves his body broken? What use is God if He cannot save the poor and the helpless? No one else sees her. No one else cares for her except ..."

The echo of his words shouted in the small chapel rang through the silence between them. It was blasphemous of him to say such things, but they came clawing up from the bitter gall in his heart.

A rustle of cloth, then Lady Wynwood was beside him, her hand on his again. "God sees her."

He shook his head wordlessly. How could he know that?

"God sees you," she said. "I do not know why you were injured, but I do know He can heal you."

The idea seeped into his mind like water into the bilges of a ship. He could be restored. "How would He do that?"

"I do not know. Perhaps in ways we cannot understand. But I have felt that healing. Miranda's calmness—the way that she calms you—that is like the peace of God that can heal you."

But without Miranda, he was not calm. He was still

angry, and frustrated, and bitter, his own unholy trinity. How could he possibly be healed?

But if God was all-powerful, then would He not see Gerard? Would He not reach him?

Lady Wynwood grasped his shoulders to turn him to face her. "Do you want to battle this for years on end?"

"No," he said, with more certainty than he had thought he possessed.

"Dear Gerard." She touched his cheek. "Even if you do not trust in the Lord Jesus Christ, I do. I know that one day, with His peace, you will once again be happy."

He had no reply for her. He did not feel much different from when he had entered the chapel. Perhaps he had expected too much. His talk with her had not changed today, and today was what pained him.

Lady Wynwood walked back down the aisle and left the chapel. Gerard remained, hands still gripping the altar, still without answers, still without an idea of what he could do.

Chapter Nineteen

Ellie was missing.

Miranda had walked back from the Lower Gardens with her and the other children, and there had been much bustling about as they shed their cloaks, scarves, caps, and mittens. The nursery smelled strongly—and not very pleasantly—of wet wool, freshened only in the corners where pine boughs were tucked.

Dinner for the children was earlier than usual today because of the New Year's Eve dinner party. The kitchen simply could not prepare the food for all the children and the grand party at the same time. But when it was time to eat, Ellie was nowhere to be found.

Miranda spent twenty minutes searching the nursery wing, in every closet and corner. She had begun to feel real concern when Jean, the under-maid, came up to her in the deserted hallway. "Miss, I found Miss Ellie."

Miranda had not seen Jean since the incident in the family wing two days ago, and her appearance now with Ellie missing made Miranda's breath freeze in her throat. "Where is she?"

"If you'll follow me, miss."

"I wouldn't follow you if you promised the way to Paradise."

Jean surprised her by stepping close to her, enough that Miranda could see the hard lines along her mouth and eyes. In a low voice, she said, "You'll come with me if you want to see Ellie again."

"If you've hurt her, you'll see what I'm capable of," Miranda said in a dark voice.

That startled Jean, and she blinked her pale eyes twice, thrice. Then they narrowed. "If you don't come with me, she'll be hurt badly."

Miranda set her jaw, then noticed Jean was wearing a cloak. "Are we going outside? Let me get my cloak." Jean looked as though she would object simply to be contrary, but Miranda added, "I will come quietly if you let me get my cloak."

Jean came into the bedroom with her as she retrieved her wool cloak, and did not object when she also snatched up her bonnet and Gerard's black and red scarf. Miranda then followed Jean down the stairs.

Michael would be helping with the preparations for the dinner party. Would they pass the dining room or the kitchens? Could she catch his eye?

But they descended to the family wing and then took the back stairs to the gardens. They saw no other servants, for they were all helping guests in their bedrooms or preparing for the dinner.

They turned toward the south end of the estate, but they did not cross the lawn, instead skirting the edge of the forest. Gerard's bedroom window faced in the opposite direction. He would never see her.

The wind had risen, and it cut through her thin cloak

like ice daggers. But her heart felt even more frozen. Was despair always so cold?

After taking a short trail through a narrow strip of woods, they came upon a dirt road used by the tenant farmers. An old traveling coach sat fifty yards away, driven by one of the men who had attacked them in the garden and at the skating party. It was the taller one, who had injured Gerard.

The coach opened and the round-faced man who had tried to take Miranda stepped out. He nodded to someone inside, and then Miranda saw Harriet.

She exited the vehicle gracefully. She had deep lines in her hard face, but her hair, visible under her bonnet, was still thick and beautiful, a rich brown color. Her eyes glittered when she spotted Miranda, but she didn't smile.

"'Randa!" Ellie's voice carried to her on the wind.

"Ellie!" She hurried forward, and now saw Ellie sitting in a corner of the coach, looking small and very cold. She had her cloak, but no mittens or cap.

Miranda had no need to say anything to Harriet. The woman helped Ellie to the ground, shoving her roughly toward Jean. She also tossed the maid a leather pouch that clinked. "My thanks, Jean." Harriet's voice was low and rough, but would sound sultry to most men.

She issued no orders to Miranda, but simply turned her blue gaze upon her and waited.

Harriet's silence was strangely frightening. Miranda climbed into the coach, and Harriet and the man followed. In a moment they were in motion, leaving Wintrell Hall far behind.

"I thought you were dead," Miranda said to Harriet.

"You probably wished I was." Idly, Harriet fingered the embroidered edge of her traveling cloak. While the material was not rich, it was of good quality, as were her gloves and bonnet trimmed in velvet ribbon. She had apparently not died a sickly prostitute, as the gossip had hinted, but had perhaps found some patron. She had the means to pay Jean, and probably these men, and to rent this traveling coach.

"Where are you taking me?"

"London." Harriet stifled a yawn.

"You're taking me to London to kill me?"

Miranda finally had Harriet's full attention. "Kill you? No. I haven't spent all this time and money to find you simply to kill you. I'll toss you into the same neighborhood where I was stranded after you had me sacked without a reference."

"You didn't deserve a reference," Miranda snapped.

"I didn't deserve anything that happened to me," Harriet hissed. "But you will."

"Why—"

"Hold your tongue or I shall have Todge cut it out for you." Harriet nodded to the man across from them. He gave Miranda a narrow gaze from eyes that were still slightly swollen from where she'd thrust her fingers into them, three days ago.

They traveled in silence for a mile. Miranda saw the forested area on either side of the road and knew they were about to leave Belmoore lands.

She knew exactly when they had to slow down because of the potholes in the public road.

She leaned down as if removing a stone from her shoe, grabbed two handfuls of dirt and straw from the floor of the coach, and flung them in Todge's eyes. Then she grabbed at the door latch and flung herself from the moving coach.

She landed hard on her shoulder, rolling on the ground and onto the side of the road. She hit the base of a tree hard enough to rattle her teeth, but she didn't pause even for breath. She scrambled to her feet, ripping the scarf from her throat to fling it aside, and plunged into the woods.

Her cloak flapped behind her, and she reached back to grasp the cloth and hold it closer so it would not catch on any branches or bushes. The wind of her passing caught her bonnet, its ribbons pulling at her throat. She scrabbled at the ends and untied it, and it flew from her head. She would be colder, but she could see more clearly around her.

Behind her came the sound of thrashing through the underbrush. She darted around the trees along a twisting path, and slowly the thrashing grew fainter.

She had to find a way to hide. What could she do?

Oh, Gerard. But Gerard may not find her.

Dear God, help me!

She had not noticed the trees around her as she ran, but she suddenly spied one that looked familiar, an old rambling oak that she and her cousins had enjoyed climbing. They had been Robin Hood's merry band, waiting to pounce on unwary travelers. They had liked the tree because although the lowest limb was above their reach, a large fallen tree trunk was nestled at the base that they could climb to reach the lowest branch.

She hiked up her skirt and scrambled up on the fallen trunk, which was taller than a table. It had protruding sharp branches that thrust straight up into the air, which she used to pull herself up, gritting her teeth against the pain in her injured shoulder. Standing on the fallen trunk, she reached for the lowest limb of the ancient oak, which was now even with her chin, and with a little hop, pushed herself up. She was not as limber as she had been at twelve, trying to keep up with Gerard, and each movement sent shafts of pain through her shoulder, but she swung her legs up, hampered by heavy skirts, to straddle the branch. She stood and continued to climb.

The branches were thick, reaching outward from the massive trunk, and ice coated the smaller limbs like white leaves. The snow rained down as she climbed higher. She lay astride a large branch far above the ground, pulling her skirts and legs up, hoping the barrel-like circumference would mostly hide her from view from below. Gerard had once hidden from his playmates by laying on his back, but she was not so brave as to flip over and release her grip on the oak.

And then she waited.

A few clumps of snow drifted down, then all was still. She strained her ears to hear Harriet or the two men, but perhaps they had stopped to listen, as well.

Oh, God, help me. She squeezed her eyes shut, resting her forehead against the cold rough bark.

But suddenly, all she could hear in her mind was Cousin Laura's voice saying, "Thou God seest me."

Why should God see her or help her? She had done a terrible thing to Harriet. She had not believed that God would care about her.

What is man, that Thou art mindful of him?

She had to believe. *Thou God seest me.*

Help me, please. Send help.

Steps picking their way slowly through the brush. Coming closer.

Miranda peeked down and realized that because the trees grew so thickly, the ground had very little snow, and was unable to give away her path through them. The steps came closer, but they were passing along the far side of the tree.

She risked another look, and her throat closed up.

Harriet was walking through the forest, one hand clutching her cloak, and the other holding a pistol.

Chapter Twenty

It was purely his foul mood that led Gerard to the library. Soon the bell would sound to dress for the New Year's Eve dinner party, but he only wanted a glass or two of Cecil's mediocre brandy.

He had never before proposed to a woman. It was just his luck that he would receive such a resounding refusal on his first attempt.

And then he'd kissed her like a desperate schoolboy.

And then she'd kissed him.

And then ...

He knew logically she had been deliberately trying to push him away, but the word had been like a blow to his stomach.

She knows how to hurt you, old chap. 'Twould be best not to get close to anyone at all.

No. Miranda might live her life by that sentiment, but he would show her that to live without love was worse.

Her kiss had simply reinforced the fact that Miranda anchored him. Home, for him, was wherever she was.

His thoughts drew him to the library windows, which was why he immediately saw Michael running across the south lawn, carrying a child.

Ellie.

Gerard hobbled out of the library and nearly broke his neck racing down the stairs.

"Captain Foremont!" Mr. Drydale sounded from the landing above him but Gerard did not stop until he met Michael in the large circular entry hall. Ellie was crying, partly from the jostling of Michael's running and partly from fear of the stranger holding her. She reached for Gerard as soon as she saw him, and he had to drop a crutch in order to take her in his arms.

"Miranda," Michael panted. "Coach. Harriet."

Ice water dashed down his spine. "Where?"

Michael shook his head. "Carriage."

Yes, they could overtake a coach with Cecil's lightest carriage. But Ellie ...

"I'll drive." Mr. Drydale suddenly appeared at his elbow. "Lieutenant, run ahead to the stables to tell the grooms. Captain, give Ellie to Laura."

Laura? Gerard looked around and saw Lady Wynwood hurrying down the stairs. "What is it?"

"I'll explain later." Gerard handed over Ellie, who went willingly to Lady Wynwood.

Michael had already disappeared. Mr. Drydale handed Gerard his dropped crutch and the two of them headed to the stables. Once there, they discovered the horses just being harnessed to Cecil's carriage, but the grooms were reluctant to saddle a horse for Michael until Mr. Drydale shouted at them.

While they waited, Michael explained, "I happened to see Miranda and a maid walking toward the forest. It looked suspicious because Miranda knows she is in danger and she wouldn't leave with only a maid. I followed and saw a strange woman with a traveling coach stopped on the south track. Ellie was already there in the coach. They traded Miranda for Ellie, as well as a bag of coins for the maid."

"That's how they got Miranda out of the house," Gerard said. "The woman was Harriet?"

"Yes. I waylaid the maid and Ellie when they headed back to the house," Michael said. "I let the maid go in order to get Ellie back here quickly. The coach is going to London."

They could still stop them. Michael had found them quickly because by the grace of God, Gerard had been at those library windows and Mr. Drydale had seen Gerard rushing down the staircase.

Mr. Drydale was the better driver and took the reins, driving expertly along the road at a frantic pace. Gerard explained about Harriet and Miranda.

"There is only one road they can take to London until they reach the turnpike road," Mr. Drydale said. "We will be able to overtake them before then."

Seated beside him, Gerard felt useless, helpless. When he was able to do something, to occupy his hands, he could focus. Now, his thoughts crowded in his mind like cackling demons. He pushed them aside with difficulty.

God help me, I can't fail her now.

And then he heard a voice that was not a voice. *She is in My hands. Be at peace.*

The demons ceased. His mind cleared.

He would find her. He knew because even though his injury had sent him back to England, it was here that he had found Miranda. The tightness in his chest eased, like the sting of a burn slowly fading.

Then they rounded a bend and saw a coach stopped along the side of the road. Michael, riding ahead of them, had already pulled up and dismounted.

"Whoa!" Mr. Drydale reined in the horses.

The coach was empty, the door open. The horses hitched to it were placid hacks who seemed only too glad for a rest and barely twitched an ear at the newcomers.

Gerard jumped down from the carriage, landing hard on his good leg and just barely preventing himself from falling by sticking out one of his crutches.

"You fool," Mr. Drydale shouted to him.

Gerard ignored him, because a flash of red and black had caught his eye.

It lay on the ground toward the edge of the woods. He knew it before he had reached it and picked it up. His scarf, the one he had given to Miranda. He looked out into the woods, but saw nothing but trees and snow and shadow.

"She escaped." Gerard couldn't help the smile that pulled at his mouth.

"They went after her into the woods," Michael said.

"Unhitch one of the gig horses. I must go after them."

"Your leg—"

"Hang my leg!"

He hadn't ridden a horse for months even before his accident, and he did not have the leg strength to guide it with his knees. But he could not make his way through the woods with his blasted crutches and he would not be left behind.

The horses were unhitched, and Gerard did not even feel a *frisson* of irritation that he needed Michael's help to slide on bareback. He hissed as the position stretched and pulled painfully at the tendons in his joint, but pointed the horse quickly toward the woods.

He rode as fast as he dared, Mr. Drydale several yards to his left and Michael on his right. Low-hanging branches nearly took his head off a few times, so he crouched down over the horse's neck. Pain pounded up his knee with each step the horse took, but he gritted his teeth and rode on. Even if he could not walk after he slid down from this horse, he would not go back until he found her.

"Miranda!" His voice sounded strangely muffled, surrounded as they were by the trees and snow. He strained it to call more loudly, "Miranda!"

Then suddenly came the sound of a single gunshot.

Chapter Twenty-One

Harriet was several yards from the tree where Miranda hid. She would walk past her in a minute or two.

Then a voice drifted through the trees. "Miranda!"

Oh no. It was Gerard.

Harriet's head swiveled around, and she searched the trees behind her. Miranda could not call to him, but she could not allow Harriet to shoot at him.

"Miranda!"

Miranda had not moved, had barely breathed, but a clump of snow from a branch above her dropped down. It collided with more snow-covered branches, and suddenly there was a cascade of snow that rained upon the ground, the only movement in the forest.

Harriet looked up. Saw Miranda hugging the tree limb. And fired the pistol.

Searing pain exploded in her shoulder. She saw stars. She felt her hands sliding over the tree bark, then forced herself to grip more tightly. But her limbs would not respond as they ought. She slid sideways on the branch and clutched at it with her legs, with her arms. Fire lanced up her shoulder.

But Harriet had fired the pistol's only bullet. She could not shoot Gerard now.

Harriet gave a wordless cry of fury. Miranda risked a glance over her shoulder and had a tilted view of Harriet throwing the pistol to the ground, then rushing toward the tree. The branch began to sway beneath her hands as Harriet climbed.

"Gerard!" Miranda began to inch farther away from the trunk, from Harriet.

Running footsteps. Harriet's two men were approaching. They would overpower Gerard.

But then she heard the sound of horses' hooves pounding through the woods, thudding with her heartbeat. Not one horse, but at least two. Possibly three?

"Miranda!" But he was still too far away.

"Gerard!" Her cry turned into a shriek as the branch she clung to dipped violently. Her hands slipped an inch but she gripped more tightly with her legs.

"Fall, you miserable—" Harriet's voice was horrible, like a pit of snakes and venom. She threw her body again at Miranda's branch.

The branch of the old oak was large all around, but Miranda had moved away from the stable trunk. The branch creaked and pitched with Harriet's weight, combined with Miranda's. She yelped as it tilted downward for an agonizing moment, then flipped upward. Her legs slid against her skirts, loosening her grip on the branch.

Harriet began inching toward Miranda along its length.

The snorting of a horse. No, at least two horses

emerging from between the trees. Men grunting, tussling along the ground.

And then the jingle of a bridle directly below her.

"Miranda, jump!" Gerard told her.

She couldn't see him, but she remembered how far away the ground had been.

"I will catch you, I promise," Gerard called.

He had said the same thing when they were playing Robin Hood in these woods. She had been trapped in the evil Prince John's tower and he'd ridden up on his pony to rescue her.

As she recalled, instead of falling into his arms, she'd bounced off the rump of the pony and then tumbled to the ground. She'd also been only half as far from the ground then as she was now. But she trusted him.

She let go of the branch.

Her shriek tore from her throat as she fell, wind rushing past her ears. Her skirts caught in some twigs, making her twist in midair so that she saw Gerard's wide eyes the moment before she collided with him. The breath was punched out of her lungs.

He swayed backward on his mount, but his arms closed tightly around her. "You're safe. You're with me."

"Gerard, move!" shouted Michael.

The horse jolted forward under her, pushing her against Gerard and making him reel backward for a moment.

There was strangely no sound, then a horrible rending thud.

"Oh, God," Mr. Drydale said.

Gerard twisted to look back, then pressed Miranda's head against his shoulder. "Don't look."

"Harriet tried to jump onto your horse," Mr. Drydale said in a weak voice. "But she did not jump far enough ..."

Miranda shuddered and buried her head against Gerard's chest. She remembered how high she'd been off the ground. She remembered the protruding branches on the fallen tree trunk that had thrust out into the air.

"Ride back," Michael said. "I'll stay here with these two. Bring some rope."

She looked toward him and saw Harriet's two men motionless on the ground.

Gerard's arms gathered her close as he turned the horse around. Miranda could feel his heartbeat next to her cheek, the rise and fall of each breath.

"It's over."

Chapter Twenty-Two

January 1st

The turret door, which Miranda always had to struggle with, opened easily under Gerard's strong hand, but it was nearly blown out of it by a whipping wind.

"It's too windy," she said. "Let's go back."

"No, Lady Wynwood said it had to be here."

"Lady Wynwood?"

She pulled her cloak around her and followed him out onto the roof of Wintrell Hall. Despite the wind, the sun shone high above, only briefly misted over by the occasional wisp of cloud before beaming down upon them, turning the red brick orange-gold.

They found a spot in the lee of the cupola where the wind was only a gentle swirling around their bodies. Gerard wrapped the wings of his greatcoat around both himself and her, and then he pulled her close to kiss her.

In the cocoon of his coat, she pressed against him, the brick parapet at her back. His mouth tasted hers, then traveled to her jaw, her neck.

"Gerard."

"Mmm."

"You did not bring me here to kiss me."

"How do you know? Maybe I wanted privacy."

"If you cared about privacy, you would not have kissed me in the middle of the drive yesterday."

After tying up the two men, they'd driven them and the rented coach to the village to turn them over to the local constable and tell him about Harriet's body in the woods. Then Mr. Drydale had driven them home in the carriage while Michael rode alongside.

Gerard had helped her down and then pulled her close to kiss her fiercely. In front of the grooms who had come racing from the stables, and the butler who had opened the front door to the house, and the family who had trickled out to see them. Felicity had given a horrified shriek that drew them apart.

"I kissed you yesterday simply to distress Felicity," he murmured into her ear. The vibration of his lips against her jaw made her shiver.

"I should have protested more before following you up the stairs just now. Your knee—"

"I submitted quite docilely to your poultice, which smelled like a pigpen, by the bye."

"It did not."

"And now my knee is 'plummy.'"

It was not. The ride on the horse had injured him further, making him lean harder on his crutches today.

"Marry me," he whispered.

"I cannot." Although that sounded ridiculous while she was in his embrace, his lips at her throat. "I have nothing ..."

He drew his head back and looked down at her, but he

did not loosen the circle of his arms. "I could not bear to lose you again. You mean too much to me."

She squeezed her eyes shut, but a tear escaped. A whistling wind turned it to ice water on her cheek. "Yes, I will marry you."

"At *last*—"

"If you will explain your reference to Lady Wynwood."

"Oh." He looked down at her, a flush creeping up his neck. "I asked her for a particular place to have this conversation with you."

"A windy rooftop?"

"It sounded romantic at the time."

She smiled at him, and he kissed her.

A few minutes later, he said, "I told Lady Wynwood that I wanted a place where you would feel loved and beautiful."

She turned toward the cupola, the glass panels gleaming. *Thou God seest me.*

"She was right."

His mouth descended on hers, his hands tightening on her back, and for a long while she drowned in sea rushes and mint and Gerard.

Connect with Camy

I hope you enjoyed *The Spinster's Christmas*! Researching Christmas in the Regency era was such a delight. If anything, the descriptions of the food made me absolutely ravenous!

I have knit Gerard's red and black scarf on my blog from an 1837 pattern that was likely in use in the Regency era. If you're a knitter, be sure to join me there: http://bit.ly/KnitGerardsScarf

There are also Book Club resources for The Spinster's Christmas and my other books on my website.

This is a prequel novel to the Lady Wynwood's Spies series, which is a Christian Regency Romantic Adventure epic serial novel.

I have another prequel novella to the series, *The Gentleman Thief,* which you can receive for FREE in exchange for signing up for my email newsletter (https://BookHip.com/DQKKMH). After a few welcome emails, I send out newsletters about once a month with a sale on one of my books, a freebie, or news about when my latest release is available.

~ ***Camy***

Made in the USA
Las Vegas, NV
05 January 2025